# The Servitude of Love

# The Servitude of Love

## Diane Glancy

RESOURCE *Publications* • Eugene, Oregon

THE SERVITUDE OF LOVE

Resource Publications
An Imprint of Wipf and Stock Publishers
199 W. 8th Ave., Suite 3
Eugene, OR 97401

www.wipfandstock.com

PAPERBACK ISBN: 978-1-5326-1773-7
HARDCOVER ISBN: 978-1-4982-4264-6
EBOOK ISBN: 978-1-4982-4263-9

Manufactured in the U.S.A.                    APRIL 6, 2017

# Contents

# Acknowledgments

"Grady and Gus"
*Parcel*

"Malchas"
*Cooweescoowee*, Rogers State University, Claremore, Oklahoma

"Minneola Peavine"
*Potpourri, a Quarterly Magazine of Literary Arts*, 2002 Council on National Literatures Fiction Award
The story of the bat is from a Muskogee story-teller, Joyce Childers Bear, who heard it from her father, Mose Childers. It is recorded as "Why Bats Fly at Night," Grandfather Stories, Traditional Cherokee Legends, Gregg Howard, Various Indian Peoples Publishing Company, 1966.

"Monkey Tree"
*Blink Again*, an Anthology of Short Fiction, Spout Press
Gratefulness to the Norbert Hill Tribal School, Oneida Nation, Green Bay, Wisconsin, for a first reading, January 13, 2004

"The Bird Who Married a Blue Light"
*Books & Culture*
*Shorelines, an Award Anthology*, Lake Superior Writers, First Place Award with a reading at The Depot, Duluth Minnesota, November 4, 2002

"The Last Indian War in Kansas"
*Front Range Review,* Fort Collins, Colorado
Gratefulness to the Kansas Arts Commission for a grant to travel the state, and to the historical markers, each giving their version of history.

"The Man Who Said Yellow"
*Image, A Journal of Art, Faith, Mystery,* No. 51, Seattle Pacific University, Seattle, Washington
*Not Safe but Good,* Vol. 2, edited by Bret Lott, WestBow Press, Nashville, Tennessee
*Bearing the Mystery, Twenty Years of Image Journal,* edited by Gregory Wolfe, William Eerdsmann Publishers

"The Only Oar You Have"
*Frontiers: A Journal of Women's Studies,* Indigenous Women's Issue, edited by Inez Hernandez-Avila and Gail Tremblay, Washington State University, for the section, "The Moon on Their Breath"
*Going to the Water,* James Wright Festival, September 29, 2000, University of Minnesota, for parts of various sections
*American Tableaux,* Walker Art Center, Minneapolis, for the section, "The Only Oar You Have," with a reading in the *Tableaux* Series at the Walker, May 5, 2002
Gratefulness to Black Bear Crossing, St. Paul, Minnesota, for a reading from "The Moon on Their Breath," February 15, 2001

"The Roundness of Earth"
*Ozone Park Journal*

"The Servitude of Love"
*Bloodroot Literary Magazine*

"The Similitude of Oxen"
*Many Mountains Moving,* with a reading at the Salon Reading Series, St. John's Episcopal Church, Boulder, Colorado, March 29, 2008
Some of the information in this story was taken from historical markers and various online sites about Kansas history.

"The Storm that Loved a Bike"
*Journal of the Humanities*, Indiana University of Pennsylvania
*Choices and Options: Interpretations of Ecclesiastes*, edited by An-
thony Pinn, Wipf and Stock Publishers, Eugene, Oregon
Gratefulness for readings to the Pima Writer's Workshop, Tucson,
Arizona, 2014
The New England Young Writers Conference, Middlebury, Ver-
mont, 2012
The University of Missouri, October 15, 2009
Fiction Collective 2, University of Florida at Tallahassee, March
27, 2006
High Plains Bookfest, Yellowstone Arts Museum, Billings, Mon-
tana, July 8, 2004

Cover art: he is the one, Murv Jacob

# THE MAN WHO SAID YELLOW

The camel, I had noticed, was passing,
with great difficulty, through the eye
of the needle.

RENATA ADLER, *BROWNSTONE*

When a great rumble of evangelism swept Brownsville, it left an unswept place around Noe as he worked in his shed. Noe was the artist, the *el artisto*, in his family. Others looked at him that way. Uncles. Cousins. Neighbors would come to look in the shed. Strangers who had heard of Noe would peer in while he worked. Often, Noe was unaware of them. His three sons started going to church with his wife. The house was abuzz with what was happening. The family had been Catholic since the Spanish invasion. Now there was an upstart *iglesia*. A church of their own.

In meetings that lasted into the night some excitement was there. It was said that angels descended and touched toothaches. Bursitis, arthritis, and cysts were healed. A baby who had coughed for days was quiet and asleep.

It was the girls that must have been at church, Noe thought. Otherwise his sons would not have been eager to go. His dreams, ah! That was the origin of art. That was his *iglesia*. That was his Maker, his *El Senor* himself—the road of open dreams. It was where he found his *yellow fever*. His *yellow works*. Canary. Finch. Yellow jacket. Noe also went to the Laguna Atascosa Wildlife Refuge. The Wetlands of Boca Chica. The Los Ebanos Preserve—for images of the wild birds, insects and small animals of his carvings, some of them surreal.

Did not the Maker speak of dreams in the Book his wife, Hesta, read to him? In a dream, in a vision of the night, he opens the ears of men and seals their instruction—Job 33:15–16. The Maker was the Maker of dreams, and not the dreams themselves. But Noe did not agree and brushed her aside.

Sometime later, there were three weddings. Not all at once, but over the year at the church, after the courtings and dinners and parties with the families, Roberto married Inez Garcia. Domingo married Cornelia Gomez. Dagoberto married Elee Padillo.

"At least his sons would not marry the daughters of unbelievers. At least they stayed away from the ungodly," Hesta said.

Now that Noe and Hesta were suddenly alone together, they didn't know what to do. Noe kept at work in his shed, carving his wooden pieces, painting them, signing them. The curators fought among themselves for his work. Noe showed his pieces and sold them at the Brownsville Heritage Museum, the Art League Museum, Imagene's Studio, and the Festival Internacional de Otoio in Matamoros across the Mexican border. There had been an article in the Brownsville newspaper about Noe's birds from the center of the earth. Another article followed about Noe's *Subterranean Cosmos*, his ingenious *Mythologies of Inner Aviaries*. Hesta sent the articles to their relatives who had gone north to Minnesota for work. She sent them to relatives still in Mexico.

Noe's work shed sat on a hill near his house with its back to the setting sun. Roberto cut a window in the shed for him and let in the evening light. After dark, Noe could work under a lightbulb in a metal reflector that caused the light to burn bright and direct on his work. In the day, when the heat came in the window, Roberto installed a canvas awning.

After several years, no children were born as yet and the three wives grieved. "There is a reason," Hesta said.

In Noe's dreams, animals began to appear two by two. When he told his wife, she was beside herself. Maybe God was getting hold of her husband at last. Maybe now he would go to church with her, just as she hoped. When Noe's two-by-two dreams continued, Hesta said, "Maybe you'll become a visionary. The end of days must be upon us," she concluded. "There is going to be a flood. Make an ark. Gather animals. That's why there have been no grandchildren."

"This isn't a ship yard," Noe said. "This is the *artisto's* shed with a tin corrugated roof"—where the grackles hopped making scratching sounds that seemed at times to direct Noe's hands.

"Then make the ark with a tin roof like your shed."

That night Noe heard camels bellow. Muffled but recognizable coming from the distance. Had he fallen asleep in his shed? Wouldn't his wife be coming to wake him or call him to bed? How could he tell? Male and female. That's what they were supposed to do. Multiply. Replenish.

That's what he did as an artist. Populate the barren world with his art.

"Camels. I see camels coming," Noe said again as Hesta took notes. "A camel train. They are bearing weight. They are with merchants, or the merchants are with them."

Eventually Noe's dreams became darker, murkier. Where did his art come from? Though camels were the central theme of his dreams, he also was flooded with images of Mexican cattle, scrawny goats, frogs, lizards, snakes, stray dogs, half-starved horses. In spite of all, he continued work in his shed, three-sided, with the fourth a large door that pushed back so that the front was nearly open to the flat brown hills.

It was as if his dreams, looking into the center of the earth for the birds that flew there, for the animals that burrowed there, had found instead, Hell. What was Hell? What was his definition? His understanding? The absence of dreams and visions? Surely such an important place should have a concept in his mind.

"Hell is when you don't know God," Hesta, his wife, said.

But Noe's theology *was* a man's belief in God. Noe just wasn't an enthusiastic and evangelistic. Noe knew the Maker, *El Senor* himself, as Himself, was there to be reckoned with at the end. Noe would live his life, do good where he could find it to do. Be faithful to his work, his art. Love his wife and family, even when he heard Inez, Cordelia and Elee scrapping.

What else could Hesta's God, her Maker, her *El Senor* himself, want?

Then why these dreams of animals? What was shaping his visions? What journey was ahead? He penciled the shapes from his dreams on a roll of brown paper. He unrolled more of the paper as he drew. He had dreamed more than he realized. What were these shapes? Camels, strange and exotic, he had never seen except in the Brownsville *Gladys Porter* Zoo.

He felt something was pulling out his eye.

His sons came of an evening with their plates of flautas and refried beans. Roberto and Inez. Domingo and Cornelia. Dagoberto and Elee, who was never ready, always late. Once, Dagoberto arrived without her. She came ambling in later, quiet and subdued, feeling shame. But she had to make certain of everything. Nothing stayed in the same place for her. Her shoes. Her little anklets edged with tatting. Whatever she needed, she had to look for. Find. Her world was watery as the Gulf and ever moving. Her dark sullen eyes moped about the room. What disarray the lives of Dagoberto and Elee would be when the children came. How loose. Unwired.

Noe continued work on his figures, painting them the yellow of a papier-mâché dog he had seen in Mexico—trying to find the essence at the core of yellow. The yellow that turned the eye into it and would not let it go. If he could look straight at the sun—he would know it. He would have it. An electrified yellow. The electrification of yellow. Even the sun could not fade it for years. The sun was what they had in Brownsville. Licking everything dry. Dulling it. The brown hills, the brown land. He lived at the bottom of the page dropping off into Mexico.

Long ago, he visited his grandparents in a *barrio* south of Matamoros in the Republic of Mexico in their adobe house. Inside his grandparent's house, where the adobe walls were a foot thick, it was cool. The house was built for the heat. Why didn't Noe have an adobe shed for his work place? Why was it a shed made of wood with a tin roof that sat out in the middle of the sun? The heat waves sometimes rose in his eyes. The whole earth wavered with Elee's indecision. What had been there in the relationship with his grandparents?—Those brilliant days. The irretrievable—the *unretrievable* past was the ache at the core of yellow.

Noe's grandfather's name had been Lamech. His great-grandfather had lived long enough that he remembered him. Whittling on wood with his bent and swollen fingers, his aching hands. His language the waltz of the gulf waves. Those days crushed in the past—those words bled yellow in Noe's memory.

The heat of Brownville. Despite the large ceiling fans in his shed. The canvas awning. Despite the spray of water he hosed over the tin roof in the early evening so he could work after supper when his family had gone to the ongoing revival at the growing church of the new *iglesia*. Where had it come from? Why had it started? Why did it continue?

Noe thought of an ark with rooms for the animals in his visions. A narrow window running the length of the ark, just under the tin roof. One door. A retractable ramp. How would the rain sound when it pecked on the roof?—Maybe a thousand grackles walking there.

Sometimes Noe still was at work in his shed before dawn under the light bulb in its metal reflector to accentuate the light. Sometimes at noonday, after lunch, he slept in a hammock in the shade of his yard until the heat subsided a degree or two and he could return to his shed as the sun began to dive into the darkness. The sun was the originator of light. The clouds were a garment over it. Garments it seldom wore. Usually it was heat and light and more heat and more light in Brownsville.

Besides camels, Noe's dreams continued with coyotes, foxes, wildcats, the fowl, the creeping things. Snakes in abundance. Scorpions. Fire ants. Termites. Brown spiders with the deadly mark of a violin on their back. How slowly he must pass over words, over visions, over those dreams to see what they were about. They were dangerous. Quick as frogs.

When sleep falls upon men, in the slumberings upon their beds—Job 33:15. He also had a troubling dream of a black angel, a Being, that roamed the hills, that had come out of the earth, that had escaped from Hell, that laid in the sun all day because of the coolness compared to Hell that drove everyone mad with thirst. When Noe told his wife, she said it was a black angel, already seen by many in Brownsville. It is what had sent everyone running to church. They were nearly on top of one another, there were so many people crowded together in the small building, and the revival kept growing. What were they going to do? Hesta said the angel was a fugitive from the wars in heaven, who now lived in the center of the earth, and would have to go back—who had somehow escaped to terrify everyone as long as it was able—and take back as many with it as it could—Just because someone didn't say Jesus Christ was Lord, Hell was laid out for them? Noe asked—Unbelievable. Unacceptable—Just Jesus without saints and priests and confession booths and candles? But *Jesus alone* was the message his wife, Hesta, brought back from church. Yes. In a dream, Noe saw someone chasing the Virgin Mary off with a broom.

His night visions continued. Bright yellow camels, not the fulvous ones in the Brownsville zoo. What was up? He had *camelitis*, someone said.

What if Noe had to build an ark not for the Flood but the Heat? "What if I dig a cellar? Submerge the ark?" Noe asked his wife one evening, wet with sweat, as they ate burritos in the yard. What if they had to flee from the heat that would flourish, that would rift, that would bake and transform the ingredients of the world? What if he was called to build a submarine? That's what they needed. The subterranean was cooler. Just step into the earth, not deep, but just beneath the surface—Weren't Domingo and Cornelia sleeping in their basement that was always cooler. Didn't Roberto and Inez join them on the hottest nights?

In the meantime, Noe wore his carpenter pouch, with his hammer in its cloth notch. He was surrounded in his work shed with metal files, clamps, drills, sandpaper, turpentine, rags, small brushes with bristles hardened with dried paint, chisels, augers, little saws with metal piranha teeth. Whatever it took to file, to whack, to form. Tubes of yellow paint, some of the letters covered with paint, which made the tubes read, *low, el,* and others simply, *yel.*

Noe also built insect cages, aviaries for an imaginary ark. He drew plans for stalls for other animals, glass cages for the creeping snakes. What was this dry flood?

*El Senor* had given exact measurements and Noe had not written them down. There Noe was *sombrero dancing* in his dreams. He was the 1840's Palo Alto Battlefield National Historical Site near Brownville. Noe was at war. He was brushed with the history of the Mexican-American War that changed the shape of both countries.

The earth was filled with violence, hunger and need. That was a clue. It was a game of Clue he had played as a boy. The game had been in Spanish. His grandfather, Lamech, had given him the game in English, so he could learn the language he needed to learn. What Clue was *El Senor* giving?

God was giving hints in Noe's dreams and Noe was losing them. His wife put paper and a pencil beside his bed. "Wake me," she said. "I'll take notes. I will do the writing. But I need measurements. Instructions. Why would they be given to you who work in your shed instead of coming to church with us? Tell me what you see." But Noe's dreams were like someone talking from underwater.

One door. Windows at the top. A tin, corrugated roof. Grackles scratching there.

Word got out. Somehow Hesta let it slip. Noe was having visions of camels, and other animals, 2 x 2. The church went wild. Cornelia said it was an aviary itself. Inez said they all would want in. How could he build an ark big enough?

His shed was an ark, wasn't it? A place of refuge in the flood of family and world events. He had sanctuary. He had replenished. But once the Flood started—if there was going to be a Flood— would they all try to crowd in his work shed as Inez said? Was it the black angel playing tricks? Was it a ghost whose purpose was to confuse?

What was he supposed to do? Noe built birds, not arks. He sat by his light bulb in its metal reflector. The insects swarmed. Did they know they would die unless they could keep flapping their wings for as long as the Flood remained? No, the rain on their wings would bring them down.

"Doors tall enough for the camels," Cornelia said.

"And the giraffes," Elee said.

Noe hadn't thought of them. And of course doors wide enough for the elephants.

What would they do as they sat in the ark surrounded by the beasts, the fowl, the creeping things? Was that what *El Senor* wanted? In Noe's night visions, the whole town sat crowded together in the ark as they waited for the rising waters. Weren't the icebergs melting and would raise the sea level? Wasn't the sea coming up to claim the land? Yes, the Gulf would rise. It would cover the Rio Grande. It already was rising, and no one knew what to do. Nightmares and Hell were giving evidence of themselves. Was the overpopulation of grackles everyone noticed like the gathering of bad spirits ready for an impending decimation? How long would they float in a Flood? But what if Noe built an ark and there was no Flood? What if, after Noe's death, his sons used the ark for a bait shop for fishermen on the gulf shore? What is his dreams were a Deluge he couldn't stop?

But there was not supposed to be another Flood. He remembered there was a promise of some sort. But Hesta seemed unconcerned.

In the night, Noe could hear the black angel rip the hills with its teeth, the mad *Being* that escaped from Hell in the center of the earth. In the afternoons, Noe walked the brown hills. Would he be the last to catch on like Elee, his daughter-in-law? As he walked the hills in despair, he was stopped as an *illegal*, but the border patrol brought him home and Hesta testified he was a citizen and her husband. Despite his family's fear of the black angel, Noe continued to walk the hills following the quavering heat waves, this time with identification. He roamed for weeks. His feet swelled. Bushes scratched his arms. He face sunburned. His children pleaded with him. When would God let her husband go, Hesta thought?

Then the Maker, *El Senor* himself, appeared, wearing a yellow poncho. For a while *He* watched the hawks. The falcons. The predators. The helicopters from the border patrol. *He* listened to the upset world with its waters rising. Once in a while, Noe looked at *El Senor*, waiting for the Maker to speak. Soon, *El Senor* announced that Hell was dreams and visions without *El Senor* attached. The

Maker said he had waited for Noe to speak *Him*. He wanted to tell Noe that he had confused his own dreams with the Maker's, the giver of dreams, just like his wife had said. What would float then was a work shed, an ark of clear vision. Noe's art was still his oar, his only hope—But if Noe would listen to the Maker's dreams—It was not an ark that *El Senor* wanted—It was a church *He* wanted Noe to build. "I want you to paint it the yellow of your birds and animals," God said, rubbing his fingers together. "I saw your work at Imagene's and the Heritage Museum. I knew I wanted it for one of my churches." It was Noe's yellow that had drawn the Maker like fly paper.

Was it all a Fluke? Or had the Creator spoken to Noe on the ankle bone of America? Yes, that was Brownsville. No, the foot bone, the toe bone just across the North American border. God had the gumption to come, then leave as quickly as he had appeared—with a trail of burros in his wake. For a moment the sky seemed to open to let *El Senor* and his burros back into Heaven, and Noe saw a light that sliced his eyes like a carving knife until he closed them.

Noe had misplaced *El Senor* in his own head where the Maker was supposed to swim on the floodwater of Noe's thoughts. Yes, Noe had seen himself as Creator. The Great and Old One. Noe fell down on his knees in the floodwaters of regret. When Noe returned to work in a heated fervor, the canvas awning blew up in a sudden storm-wind and the work shed looked like it had a sail— The townsfolks came to watch. They knew Noe had a vision. What was he building? No, he was drawing—he was drawing plans for their church. In the end, the *El Senor* was going to enlarge the *iglesia*—It's what they prayed for, Hesta reminded them. Noe saw the dimensions in his dream. This time he wrote them down. Noe, the repentant *artisto*, would be used to build a church or draw it and show others how to build or help build. The animals in his dreams had been the people, burden bearers, workers, men and women who carried the weight of their families—also the hungry, the sick, those who needed sanctuary, those who had been scorpions—who had wounded others and now sought redemption.

The ark was the *El Senor Himself*, his wife said as the family gathered with their stuffed peppers, their chili rellanos, and refried beans. Sometimes mystery turned up like a canvas awning. The ark was a type, a metaphor for safely on the floodwaters of the world. Once in an everlasting while, some dust blew up in the heat, stirred by the winds from heaven, and left a puddle of revelation—a downpour of sorts on a level Noe had not expected, nor even desired.

# MINNEOLA PEAVINE

Ride whan yow list, ther is namoore to doone.

"THE SQUIRE'S TALE," *CANTERBURY TALES*,
GEOFFREY CHAUCER

She dreamed of Genghis Khan the night she married.

Afterwards, she moved into her husband's house. Gun-pow-der. A printing press. The usual.

She continued to dream of Genghis.

There were irreconcilable differences. She was American. He was a Hun. She was someone else's wife. He was a war lord. She never asked Genghis to leave. She never asked why he'd come.

By the first year of her marriage to Weston Peavine, she was riding with Genghis nightly across Mongolia. She could smell the smoke from the campfires. She could hear the war plans.

She liked the muffled sounds the tents made when they collapsed to the ground. She loaded the pack animals when they broke camp. She liked the jingle of the horses' bridles when the army moved across the desert. Maybe it was the hunger for her own ancestors who had been the *barbarians* of America when the U.S. Cavalry came.

Their differences continued. She was born in 1964 in Texas. He was born in 1165 somewhere on the border of Siberia and Mongolia.

She lived after the Age of Enlightenment. He, before.

She was raised in a large family in relative comfort. He was raised by his mother in hardship after his father was poisoned by the Tatars.

When Minneola ate with Weston, her husband, at Sluggy's, a new wave Chinese restaurant, she blushed when she read her fortune:

*If people were barbarians, you'd ride with Genghis Kahn.*

How did Genghis cross the Pacific the nights he came to her? Did the Bering Strait come together for him? Did his army fly on a cargo plane?

At night, there were animals from the Gobi desert in her backyard. The camels and horses, the sheep and goats, the guard dogs and llamas. The yaks. She didn't know what to do. She could see the daxxle of the night sky. Dazzle, she meant. But the words came out contorted. Why couldn't she just go live with him? There were differences, yes, but Genghis showed her the sky. There were more stars where he lived. She could hear them growling. Why were there noises in the stars? From her backyard, she saw them as torches of the Mongolian army on the move.

She lived in Texas with her husband, Weston Peavine. But she also traveled to Mongolia. How could she tell her husband she had a tent? A flock of goats? How could she tell Weston her arms ached from carrying the water jugs from the well?

What did she do in Mongolia anyway? You know. Go into battle. Conquer. Pillage.


The Peavine family was from the hill country of West Texas where their well-water tasted like sulfur. They had migrated to land near Fredericksburg.

Minneola had gone to the University of Texas, where she studied medieval literature. She always had liked crusades and pilgrimages. It was where she met Weston.

Now he had a harness and bit store that carried western ware. He called it, Double XX.

A twice-divorced friend called it, the Double EX.


At night, Genghis waited in the mesquite along the river until Weston slept.

Minneola read Genghis the Squire's Tale in her dog-eared copy of the *Canterbury Tales*. Heere bigynneth the Squieres Tale— a kyng cleped Cambyuskan, which was Genghis. He was hardy, wys, pitous and riche. He had a wife named Elpheta. Two sons named Cambalo and Algarsyf. A daughter, Canace. They ate heron chicks and roasted swan.

She wondered how to say, Algarsyf, turning it over and over in her mouth to call him in from the horses.


The Peavines became regulars at Sluggy's.

If people were cars, you'd be a Chevy Nomad.

When Weston wasn't looking, she put her tongue on the fortune after she read it. When he wasn't looking, she bit off a corner. Why? She hoped it would impregnate her and she would bear Genghis' children.

Minneola loved the Gobi plateau. The scarps of central Asia where Genghis overran the Asiatic and European continents. He conquered China and Russia. He conquered the Yellow Sea, the Baltic. The wind blew all year, and the dust storms. In the winter, they rode in the frigid cold. The land was barren except for the larch and spruce woods near the rivers, a few grasslands for the flocks. The Mongols lived mostly in the saddle. She had to get used to it at first.

Genghis explained the Mongols sang their way toward the mountains, their voices rising and falling with the peaks. They carried no map, only a song of the place they were headed. He explained they changed the directions with their song. They sang their way south no matter which direction they traveled.

When they camped, she unfolded the heavy felt blankets over the frame-work of a tent and tied the bottom of the blankets to large stones. She pounded silver for her head-dress. She wove a goat-hair blanket for Genghis.

When they moved, she drove the goats with a long stick. She wanted to tell Weston all this as they ate at Sluggy's.

The tents and yurts in Mongolia had sloping roofs with a hole in the top to let out the smoke of her cooking fire. The ranch house in Texas also had a sloping roof that covered the front porch. Inside the ranch house was a large room with a beamed ceiling. A wide-plank floor. Stone fireplace. Rag-braided rugs. Tables with beaten tin work. Book case. A broad, leather sofa. Some of her

Indian artifacts. A goat hair blanket from Mongolia. The cowhide chairs with lone-star pillows embroidered, 1845, the year Texas became a state.

Then there was the dirt yard, the farm-to-market roads bordered in bluebells, the Pedernales River, the wind, the wild screech of land. Farther away, the escarpment of hills, the blackland prairies, the yellow pine forests, the Balcones fault line. Like Mongolia, Texas was so vast a man could get lost in it, unless he drove stakes in the ground to find his way back.

Weston had a marauder at the Double XX. A clerk was taking money. Weston fired him. For a while he stalked the Peavines, hiding in the bushes. Minneola thought she saw him when she drove the farm-to-market road to Fredericksburg, along with an occasional coyote, wolf or bobcat. She hoped he didn't run into Genghis. Finally Minneola's five brothers formed a posse and scared the marauding clerk out of Texas for all she knew.

In the afternoon, Minneola helped Weston arrange the Double XX, and unpack new shipments of western ware. She ordered more lone-star pillows. He liked her taste. Her sense of placement.

A yurt could be dismantled in half an hour.

When they traveled, the Mongols found places for their villages near wells. They also found places protected from the great winds of the plains. They made corrals for the goats near their tents; they kept the horse and pony herds further away. The Mongol children collected the dung for campfire in their nearly treeless country. Their fierce dogs drove away the wolves.

Minneola and Weston drove to Fort Worth for a Davis family reunion.

Her great-grandfather, Woods Davis, displaced from Oklahoma, had been a drover. Her grandfather, Claude Justice Davis, was a small rancher, a farmer, actually. Her father, Matthew, worked in the stockyards in Fort Worth where he became foreman. Her brother, Paulo Davis, had a meat market in San Angelo. Her other brothers, Houston, Zachary, Wells and Warrick, rodeoed.

Her brothers had wives and children. Their names floated everywhere in the air at cook-outs. Weldon. Ware. Macklin. Ledyard. Kirk. Justin. Albert. Guston. Colton. Roy. Mettabel. Matty. August. Felda. Fritta. Catherine. Calla. Saint Clare.

Why did Minneola dream of Genghis? Maybe it was growing up in a world conquered by five brothers. Maybe it was her connection to the Indian world of her people that had moved before this one.

The high grasses. The pasture land. A yurt here and there. Texas could be its own country, Genghis told her. They could build a wall around Texas to keep others out. Except for trux that had to pass along the interstates, she said.

Texas had been its own nation, Minneola told him, before it became a state. The Texas flag was the only flag that could fly at the same height of the American flag. Texas had seceded over slavery, but applied for readmission to the union. She didn't think they'd secede again.

She liked the rocking camel-ride along the trade routes where the Mongols bartered for sugar and tea. It was easier than riding the Mongolian horses. It was easier than walking with the goats.

In the afternoons, she continued to drive to Fredericksburg to the Double XX, or to Lusty's, the grocer.

In some of the books she read, Genghis' three sons were named Jugi, Jugatai and Ogotai or Ogdai. But wasn't one of his children, a daughter? Minneola didn't like the changing, shifting language. She didn't like the way words moved around like checkers on a board. Like checked curtains in the breeze. Or checkered. Or was it chexed curtains in the breexe?

What if her brothers turned up with new names every time she saw them? What if her own name changed? She could sign a new name to her check the next time she went to Lusty's. Hadn't there been enough changes? She remembered learning to write her name, Minneola. The double horseshoes of the *n*'s. The open moon of the *o*. The corral of the *e*. She was named after two great aunts, Minnie and Leola Davis. Two sisters who had never married. Her name, Minneola Davis Peavine, was a certainty in a turbulent world that had the upheaval of five brothers just under the wind.

Minneola was born with a pink little fist her mother unfolded with a kiss.

Genghis was born with a piece of clotted blood in his hand. A seer prophesied he would be a conqueror. What a vocation.

Genghis' father ruled 40,000 tents until he was murdered.

Her father left the open range and ruled 10,000 cattle in the stockyards. He had bent his life to fit the new world. Couldn't Genghis do the same?

Genghis united the Mongols. Her father fought the unions, breaking them up, though, in the end, the unions prevailed.

The Mongolian tableland in Central Asia. The plateau of Texas. Maybe they weren't so different after all, she thought as she pick-axed her way back across the Bering Strait to Mongolia at night.

Minneola missed the movies when she was in Mongolia. She missed television. She tired of story-telling each night. She had told Genghis 1) 187 men died fighting at the Alamo in 1836. 2) She told him of the massacre of Goliad a few days later when Sam Houston, commander of the army of the new Republic, defeated the Mexican army. 3) In 1847, Generals Winfield Scott and Zachary Taylor invaded Mexico and captured Mexico City. With the Guadalupe-Hildago treaty, the Mexican claim to Texas was relinquished.

Genghis liked the stories of conquest. 4) A few years later, in 1861, Texas seceded on the side of slavery. 5) In 1866 they reapplied for readmission as a state, renouncing right to secession and slavery in their new constitution. 6) By 1870, Texas was a state again.

Wasn't there a Gobi, Texas?

A rattler crawled into Wells' pick-up and bit him on the arm when he reached for his saddle. He died before they could get him to a hospital. Minneola drove her car in a fury across the Texas plains.

Paulo pulled the family through.

By then, Minneola was expecting her first child. The baby was born the following December. She wanted to name the baby after her brother, Wells, but Weston didn't like the name. Then she thought of Paulo, but Paulo didn't go with Peavine. Maybe with another name between Paulo and Peavine. Paulo Weston Peavine. Paulo Genghis Peavine. It was Peavine that was causing the trouble. Eventually, Weston agreed to call him, Wesley Wells Peavine. He was a ruddy baby who frowned as he ate.

Minneola didn't know if he was Genghis' or Weston's.


There were arguments at a neighbor's late into the night. Several times the wife knocked on the Peavine's door for refuge. Often the sheriff's car was in the yard. The woman would have to leave him.

One night the neighbor ran to their house and her husband followed. He rushed into the room and beat his wife, shredding the 1845 lone-star pillows.

Weston tried to subdue the man. There was fury between them. Weston wrestled with the man until he broke Weston's ankle. The woman's screams indistinguishable from the arriving siren.


Minneola was expecting again. Another son was born. Minneola named him Tait.

The next day, as Weston stepped from his store, there was an accident in front of the Double XX that killed two boys.

Weston was despondent. He wouldn't hold the baby. He was afraid something would happen to it.

"You can't stand back," Minneola said. "You have to hold him."

But Weston withdrew into his work. Horseshoes and barb wire.

THE SERVITUDE OF LOVE

Three more children were born. Charles, Rosa, and Claude, named after her grandfather who wore small round glasses on the end of his nose.

How could she handle all this and Mongolia too?

In her spare time, she made a little cap for the hawk Genghis took when he hunted. The little caplet came down over its eyes so the hawk couldn't see where it was going until it got there. She also sewed a heavy yak-hide mitten for Genghis' arm and hand when he carried the hawk.

One evening, Weston watched her sew. "You're like food tied in a tree the bears can't get to," he said.

"Are there bears in Texas?" She asked.

"Sometimes you're far away," Weston said. "Sometimes I think I could catch up if I tried, but you always get ahead."

Minneola bit the thread with her teeth.

Now the stars at night were xxx's from Genghis. Sometimes they seemed to bark from the dark sky. One night at Sluggy's, her fortune read, *Eat my dust.* She would continue to commute to Mongolia and back, xing the ocean, croxxing out all that was behind her. She would continue to do what there was to do.

Minneola read *The Squire's Tale* to the children in Mongolia.

*Ther is no fowel that fleeth under the hevene that she ne shal wel understonde his stevene* (speech). Yes, in Mongolia, Minneola could understand the flush of birds from the scarp. She could understand the llamas. The lleaves that fell from the llarch trees.

There were so many grackles around the Pedernales River, the water became polluted with their droppings. She tried to explain the word, polluted, to Genghis, who would not believe what happened to the earth.

Locusts. Fire ants. Snakes. Scorpions. West Texas was similar to the Gobi desert.

The rodeo horses rode across Texas in their horse trailers. They were prepared for battle in their saddles and cinches. Genghis laughed when she tried to explain the transport of animals in trailers.

She tried to explain tornados, western dust storms, lightning balls, electric disturbances, radio static always on the edge of the world. There were times they simply couldn't communicate.

The Peavines often took the family to Sluggy's. The children didn't like Chinese, but Minneola wouldn't listen to their protests. She loved the Chinese waitresses. In their faces, she could see the descendants of the Mongols. In the restaurant, she could communicate with Genghis. When the children weren't looking, she took all their fortunes. The children were usually fighting or crying by then. She read them later at night when Weston was asleep. She put a corner between her teeth. What if they found her teeth marks and measured her mouth against it? She didn't want that to happen. She put the whole strip in her mouth. She chewed the fortunes, and when they were a glomp in her mouth, she swallowed them whole.

One Sunday, a tornado unwound from the sky and blew the Double XX from Texas.

Horseshoes, stirrups, saddles, bits, probably in Oklahoma and Nebraska. Who knows where they fell from the sky.

Weston was daxed. Dazed, rather, but not hurt.

Minneola hurt her arm running to the cellar with the children, bruised it or cracked it, but after an x-ray, she discovered it was broken. Or the doctor did, rather.

But all five children were unharmed.

Afterwards, it rained for two weeks, swelling the creek over the road. She heard frogs croak she hadn't heard in years.

Two Mexican girls who did her housework and tended the children couldn't get through.

She felt like Minneola, the Dishbite.

Eventually the sun baked the land white. The air was raspy with dust, and the Mexican girls returned to work. The arid air dried the joints of her leather sofa and plank floor. She had the Mexican girls oil the furniture and floors.

Eventually, Weston got the Double XX rebuilt.

Then it was Xmas.

The winter sky was branded with stars as they drove to Fort Worth with their five children.

Every year, they went to Paulo's house. Every year, the Davis family gathered: her grandmother, the widow of Claude Justice Davis, Minneola's father, her brothers, Houston, Zachery, Warrick, their wives and children, and Wells' widow and children. The women cooked in the large kitchen. The younger children played upstairs. The older ones talked outside, unless it was too cold.

It was the one time she felt disconnected from Genghis. He wouldn't come near her family.

After Xmas Genghis was waiting. She loved his xanthous skin.

What was this illness? The symptom of which was the appearance of the letter x in her words. She ordered TexMex at the Chinese restaurant. She set the Mexican girls to polishing and rubbing the furniture as though they could rub away the x's she saw everywhere. But she found more x's under the bed, behind the chest, in the children's toys. She began seeing only x's on the pages of the *Canterbury Tales*. Weston thought it was the stress of all the children and hired another Mexican girl.

Minneola was xerophilous. She could flourish in the dry, hot environment of Texas, and the summers of Mongolia. Or could she?

She suffered from xerosis, an extreme dryness of her skin, and oiled her body nightly.

She heard Genghis' xiphi clacking against the armor of the enemy.

"Don't you ever stop fighting?" Minneola asked him. "Can't you sit quietly and do something? Carve. Take up the hobby of xylography?"

He looked at her.

"Or take your xyster and scrape some bones?" She finished, feeling an ache in her arm that had been broken during the tornado.

She told her doctor about her travels in Mongolia. It was the temporary stress of all those children.

"Get a grip," he told her.

The stars were groaning again. Someone was walking across them, or maybe the wood floors of her house. Wesley, Tait, Charles, Rosa or Claude when they climbed into her bed at night after a bad dream. Maybe it was just the overlap of her worlds, everything moving together like travelers on a pilgrimage.

"I saw my parents live separately in one house," Weston said. "I don't want that, Minneola."

She picked a bouquet of bluebells and put them in the Weyman's powder-white snuff-jar from an antique stall that her sister-in-law had given her.

"Our house has to be someplace you want to be."

"I want to be here."

"But you aren't," Weston insisted.

"Leave me alone," she said.

"I want a wife. Not someone I should leave alone. Where are you?"

"I am here."

"I see an elbow," Weston said. "A jaw. The toe of a shoe. But not you. Hire another Mexican girl if the children bother you. We could go to Mexico for a vacation. You can work at the Double XX if you want out of the house."

She wanted to x-it. Croxx it out. Shut the door. Never come back.

She knew she should sing her marriage into being, her voice fluttering over the rise of peaks. Instead, she headed northwest, across the ocean to Mongolia.

Minneola read the *Canterbury Tales* to her own children until they ran when they saw her coming with the book.

One night she listened to a story the Mexican girl read the children. It was from a book of American Indian stories Minneola kept in the book case. The story was about a bat named Glah-may-ha, who argued with the birds he was a bird because he could fly, and was allowed to sit in their council. Then the animals held a council, and guess who argued that he was an animal.

"Glah-may-ha," said Wesley Wells Peavine, frowning with seriousness.

"Glah-may-ha," said Tait.

"Glah-may-ha," said Charles.

"Glah-may-ha," said Rosa, pushing Claude away from her.

"Glah-may-ha," said Claude.

"Glahx-may-hax," said Minneola.

"Yes," said the Mexican girl. "It was the bat."

He told the animals that he was a mammal because he had fur and teeth. He was allowed to sit in their council, though they eyed him from the side. When the birds heard Glah-may-ha sat in the animals' council, they said, you cannot be a bird. When the animals heard Glah-may-ha sat on the birds' council, they said, you cannot be an animal. So Glah-may-ha flies alone at night.

Minneola listened to the story the Mexican girl read from the book of Indian stories. Minneola knew she was the bat, not part of any world. No, she was a border walker. Not belonging anywhere, but traveling between the borders of light.

Minneola thought about the story when the children were in bed, and Weston had not yet returned from the Double XX, and Genghis was out warring.

When the children were asleep, she made wings for herself. She cut into a blanket with her pinking shears, making serrated edges like little x's so she could traverse the world, hooking the wings to her wrists and ankles with cuffs. She was not a bird or an animal, but an outcast flying in Mongolia or Gobi, Texax.

If she could just focus, for once in her life. If she could just see with a single vision—

She heard one of the children crying, maybe with an earache or a bad dream. She went into their bedrooms in her bat wings. It was Rosa. Minneola held her in the chair, covering her with the wings.

She heard Weston come in the door.

"Minneola?"

"Shhuuuu," she whispered when he was at the bedroom door.

When Rosa slept again, Minneola returned to the main room of the ranch house.

She found Weston on the leather sofa.

"What are you wearing?" He asked.

"Bat wings."

She sat in a cowhide chair with a lone-star pillow at her back, one of the pillows she had replaced after the neighbor ripped the other ones fighting with his wife. No, it was Weston he had struggled with, breaking Weston's ankle. Sometimes Weston limped when he came in late from working at the Double XX.

"Your bat wings look like one of the imported blankets we sell at the store," Weston said.

"They are," she answered.

Weston hit the floor with his feet. He stood above her. "I assume you have lost your mind. Gone batty." He understood how his neighbor could rip up a house because of his wife. He wanted to send Minneola to Mongolia. "What's the matter with you, Minneola?"

"I'm spending time in Mongolia," she answered. She could wear her bat wings there and Genghis would not complain.

What now? Weston hit the wall with his fists. He had five children and an unstable wife. An unreliable narrator. He had the Double XX, and a sister in Tucson whose husband was on the edge of leaving her. He saw the devastating effect of the disruption on his nieces. He was responsible for the peaceable lives of his children and wife. Weston Peavine would tighten the cinch. He would stay aboard his horse, and ride out the silliness. Put it behind him. He would be practical. But life with Minneola was a difficult ride. She went someplace he couldn't follow. Didn't want to follow. Wasn't invited to follow. He couldn't grasp where she went. Where she was when they sat at supper in the ranch house. What could he do? Surrounded as he was by the branding irons and barbed wire of her head. He stormed around the large, main room of the ranch house.

He pounded the floor with his feet long enough that a neighbor heard him, the neighbor who had flung himself into Weston's house. Weston apologized for the noise and hung up the phone. What if his despondency returned? He was agitated. He had come close to brutality and Minneola was the one who had nearly sent him there. No, they each were responsible for their own destiny, leaving behind their cluttered lives like flies on a horse blanket. Weston holding onto a corner of the Double XX. Minneola, hoping that Genghis would be there, holding a glass of goat milk for him under her bat wing.

# THE BIRD WHO MARRIED
# A BLUE LIGHT

maaizhaa gaye mikwamiin awiiya iidog gegishkawaagen—

the ice he must bear within himself

When Aazhawakiwenzhiinh Almost Became a Windigo

Maude Kegg

FROM NOOKOMIKS GAA-INAAJIMOTAWID
WHAT MY GRANDMOTHER TOLD ME

And the same man had four daughters, virgins, which did prophesy.

—ACTS 21:9

Our Lady of the Curlers. That's what we call Agoba, our sister. Her boyfriend is the unwanted lover of the lake. He calls to each wave and speaks to ships and freighters gone to their watery graves. Cordelio's family came north for work. Sometimes on Sunday morning, Cordelio goes to Mass at the Catholic Church with his family. The cold, the cold is a god, he says. Cordelio calls the snow, angels falling. There's no one left in heaven to do God's work, he worries. But God's work is done on earth, my father tells him. We snatch the lost from the fire—Jude 23. We are a blemish on Agoba's love feast. We sit in church and hear the testimonies—I chopped one tree shared the wood with my neighbor had wood all winter. I was in the lion's mouth. I was in the whale's belly and he spit me out on the shore at Little Marais. A church family has its trials just like others. Pentecostal Christianity is no guarantee against trials, though my father spells it *trails* in his sermon notes. When Agoba translates his handwriting into readable sermons, she corrects his misspellings.

Agoba was my father's grandmother's name. He thought it was anyway. Agoba hoped so, suffering as she did with that name all her life, she said. We call her Agie. Over that she has suffered as well. She won't speak for herself. Meekness is her mark—her cross to bear. It's what she says anyway. There are four of us—all sisters. Dunlin, Juna, Phoebe and Agoba. Our father is the preacher in the Waters of the Superior Church, the kind with signs and wonders following.

I, Dunlin, called Dunie, or Dumie sometimes by the sisters, am named after a plover, a shore bird which nests on the ground at the intersection of blue sky, blue water and the blue distance of the north woods. It also was a family name—my father thought his grandfather's name was something like it. Phoebe is a Biblical name. Juna is named after no one. The four of us are a year apart. We look nearly the same except Agie was given Hair. My father's grandmother was known for the hair she kept tied like a freighter to the dock. But when she let it loose, it sprang from her head in masses. The Hair hit every other generation, and only one girl in that generation. Agoba was the Chosen. She fluffed it, brushed it, curled it, and she outshone us. None of us had hope of any one sitting on the front pew with us as long as Agoba was not taken. One boy, who couldn't make up his mind between Juna and Phoebe after Agie wouldn't have him, was soon gone. We lost our patience. Though Agie had all the boys, she wanted only Cordelio. She wouldn't leave the house until her Hair was curled and she looked like an angel flown down from heaven. Our Mother of Sorrows. Our Father of Mystery. Our Holy Spirit of Many Tongues. Our Sisters of Manifest Density.

My father also holds tent revivals in Croftville, Hovland, Tofte, and other places along the north shore; some of the churches no bigger than an ice-fishing house, and just as cozy with a wood-stove and a hot plate, a few rows of pews with holders on the back for hymnals and Bibles, some lace tatting at the windows for curtains made by the old ladies. Sometimes we go as far inland as Isabella. Biwabik. Other towns from which names have been forgotten. A long line in the mass of the forgotten. All hoping they don't run us out. You see my father had a vision some time back at the church. One Sunday morning he saw the church was failing— was remiss in not getting Jesus' word out to people. Side-stepping the gospel message—Are you saved by the blood of the Lamb? That to him was the central core. The glacial plate of unbelief had to move off the north country.

We have a camper we park behind the church. Sometimes we hit the state parks where my father preaches over his loud speaker to the campers. Sometimes I want to jump off Gooseberry Falls.

Juna calls to the lake—Precious one, I have dreamed of you out where the moon strays over Superior—you know you are my sweet one—let's dance in the dark and not tell anyone—most of all my father—hold me as a light to your body—it is what I am made for—

That is Juna—All she wants is a boyfriend more than life itself. She'll jump from the lighthouse on Split Rock Point or whatever cliff she can find—if not into the lake to drown forever—she'll marry the waves. That's Juna who received fish bait for a brain at birth.

Only the Holy Ghost keeps her alive. I hear my father's prayers until they are red as masabi from the iron range—that raw ore in Minnesota that ships take away. It is all and everyday my prayer, O Lord, that you keep my daughters pure—let the boys look elsewhere with their desires. My father will not allow it, will not let his daughters give themselves until they are wives. My father the dreamer.

In church we make up names for our boyfriends—St. Lars, St. Bill, St. Jake, St. Cordelio for Agoba.

Nearly everyone is Catholic, but that doesn't stop my father who holds out for the gospel without a denominational banner. Christ alone is our fortress. It is his revelation. We are along for the ride. But we have to pull our weight, so to speak. We prophesy, which women are allowed to do in church. Not preach, though Agie would be good at it. But we are charismatic Christians. Filled with the Holy Ghost. Once I had a vision of the aborted babies crying out like honeybees buzzing the hive of the unwanted. I was sick for days afterwards saying, Holy Holy. How can we do that knowing the soul has wings that cries forever for its life?

It's a grim note, those birds with open beaks in the heat. We have it sometimes here along the shore. Heat. Spell that for me, please, Cordelio says, I've forgotten.

Sometimes I'm given a hundred visions a day. They are like dreams passing—partial ones not given full life. Those baby-parts like milagros on the altar before God. Those birds flying above the shore in the sky. Sanctus. Sanctus. Sanctoose.

What would you let go of? My father preaches. What is holding you back from running the race? Grief. That's what came to mind. Grief? What do I have to grieve? All the voices in the grieving world. I pick them up somehow. I was born with hornlets on my head. Sometimes Juna sees them at night where horns would be if I were a deer. She calls Agie and Phoebe to feel them while I sleep. Not that animal transformations aren't a part of the faith. But not in everyday acknowledgment.

Don't you want a son-in-law? We asked our father. Don't you want another man in the house? You live with women. Don't you get tired of being the only man? But his prayers never helped as far as any of us knew. In fact, they seemed to drive the men off. Don't you want grandchildren? Don't you want to see us wives and mothers of children? He answered that he did and we searched his face with the spirit eyes in our head, and it seemed he was saying he did. But his prayers, if they were prayers, never were answered. Once Juna got to crying and didn't stop until the next day. Mother kept making her drink water. Otherwise she'd dry up. When it's darkest, you see the blue light of the word, my father said.

My father was from a large family. They lived near Soudan along highways 1 and 169—the one highway having two numbers, highway 1 coming north from Lake Superior to Ely where it joined 169 from nowhere, and together they traveled to a point four miles west of Soudan where they separated. My mother was an orphan, raised by an aunt near Ely. The story was that my mother's parents parted like the highway and she never saw them again. It was for the best, she said, though I don't think she believed it. My father said sometimes he could see the blue light of sorrow in her eyes. She made up names for her parents—Joseph and Mary. We laughed when she told us and she seemed hurt.

On one trip she decided we should memorize the names of the ten thousand lakes in Minnesota. With six of us, that made 1,666 names each, or close to it, all the lakes made by the hoof-prints of Paul Bunyan's blue ox, if you believe that. If Cordelio would travel with us, we would be down to 1,428. If the four of us all had boyfriends, we would each have 1,000 lakes to memorize. We started with the major lakes—Superior, Lake of the Woods, Lower and Upper Red Lake, Leech Lake, Winnebigoshish, Mud Lake, Mille Lacs and Vermillion. I don't remember how far we got after that.

Sometimes we stop at campsites along the Temperance River or Manitou State Park. Sometimes we stop at Bear Head State Park near Vermillion near the Iron Range. We pull up at campsites where several tents are pitched. Then on Sunday morning my father lets it rip with the guitar my sister, Phoebe, plays. The campers look up in the wilderness as if startled at first. I wish I could say I was embarrassed, and would leave with the first motorcyclist or camper who wanted another girlfriend or grown child or wife, if there was a Mormon in the park. But there is joy in being in the Lord's presence. I actually can feel it—A Holy Someone who stands with us. The campers ignore us, or try to look pleased while holding one eye on the road for my father to take his first breath so they can make their escape. I can't say that we saved anyone. We helped a man with a broken tent once, and we've given money sometimes instead of taking an offering. We even found a family camping in the woods because they couldn't afford to live in town. We let them stay in our camper behind the church, but they finally moved on.

It's grief I pick up—those gone ones. Those who had the land before the preachers and their congregations. Yes, I think it's Indian voices that lived without the message of salvation. The ice they carry within. Sometimes we leave feelings behind that others pick up. Sometimes I feel they are eating me with their grief. I snap as if a communion wafer.

At times, even Cordelio seems to move away from us. What is it like to prophesy? He asks. I never know what I say until I speak. I have to give myself to it. I feel the silence and the silence opens my mouth. Then words are there, words of another language, I don't know what language, I don't know what the words say, but I speak. Then someone interprets, gives the message in English.

There's a blue lizard living in me that plays the base guitar, I tell Cordelio. I open my mouth and prophesy. The words are like herds of different animals—moose, wolf, bear, badger, beaver. That was the message once—it was from the animals in heaven. They were all right. We didn't need to grieve. They didn't remember their painful deaths by arrow or gunshot or trap. Then I picked up a message from a bird flying over. It spoke old voices just under the ledge of civilization.

My father glared at me from the pulpit.

I had a message from the animals, I tell him afterwards. I say what I receive.

I don't think animals come into the kingdom of God.

I think they do! I said.


It was one of our major disagreements. That and there is no shame in being the father of four unmarried daughters!!!!

Yes, watch out for your sons. They'll be hogtied behind our camper and dragged off for one of the sisters. We would have shot anyone who said that, even thought it, though you could tell what they were thinking the way they looked at us as though we were manitous with a taste for blood. One minister started to say something in a church we visited once. You can imagine us on the front row turning scarlet, burgeoning with shame. He had no more sense than a muskrat. He had us trapped with no escape. But we are unmarried women. Women without men. *Birgins*—all of us, though we look at Agoba with one eye. Some would call us lucky. I've seen plenty of unhappy wives wondering how they got into what they were in. We were blessed in their eyes. Nothing like being stuck with a husband you feel your love for drifting away like the sweet smell of bread out of the oven that turns to a hard block if left on the counter a couple of days. Even an ax won't cut it and you're married to it for life. Even salvation doesn't cure the blot that marriage makes. The children one after one until you figure out how to stop them, and by then you're in for three or four or five. Some of the women feel they chop firewood that just keeps coming.

Our Lady of the Curlers nearly caught one. Cordelio seemed everything he was not, just up from Mexico with us into diversity and inclusiveness of other cultures and he with his cross and belief in the saints and ave marais. He could pray silently to himself longer than anyone in that church cluttered with icons and apostles and saints. How could anyone else get in the door?

It was easy to see Cordelio from the barrio where they have '57 Chevy's with dice hanging from the rear-view mirror, the car weighted in back or front, full of guys with their black hair slicked back. Agie thought Cordelio was hers, but St. Cordelio transformed under the weight of the ice, and joined the ethereal, the invisible, the never present St. Jake, St. Lars, St. Bill. In church, I prophesy—He is ice that melts and disappears with the winter. For a while Agoba hung around the Catholic Church on her cross, but we dragged her back. Then she grieved in silence.

We will marry the sky, I tell Agoba. There is enough of it for everyone. Remember the mystery of the five loaves two fishes that fed the multitudes with twelve baskets of bread left? We're still puzzling over that one. But we have driven to a town without enough gas to get there, by my father's calculations, who has been calculating gasoline for some time.

When you are born again a new life opens somewhere under the ribs and fills your head with a wave that is Christ himself. The water grows inside you and you get puffier with the new life until you shuck the old body and you are his new being.

We have been undone by waiting. Even Agoba's hair seems wilted. By knowing the second birth, the lion's den, the marching band, the mariachi band, the illuminata of the Waters of the Superior Church of Our Glory of the Risen One, and the dimming hope we would have husbands, the desert turns to snow. We stay low in winter. The roads nearly impassable in bad years. A few Sundays, there's no one in church but us. A few weeks, there's only beans and bread on the table. In good years we get from here to there. My father is a circuit rider in a camper, taking the wife and the four daughters with him. The daughters being—Agoba of the Hair, Phoebe of the Guitar, Juna of the Fish Brain, Dunlin of the Plover Tongue—as though by taking us around the state he would make us visible to more men. The more we saw the fewer there were to see. They seemed to know we were coming and cleared out to the Boundary Waters or even Bemidji. Some had been known to leave for Canada.

But what came from our travels, looking at the blue map, was a story, as if heard through the hornlets Juna saw on my head. The voices of the land, the Indians who lost the land, the first settlers, the poor, the cold, whoever knew what it was to lose their place in line—transformed into birds who traded their places in the trees for the open spaces of God, who would fly upward and upward into the blue light that God is, who goes on and on forever, as if the map reflected what was above it—the story of our migration into the blue light of sorrow which we call heaven, and whosoever believed in Jesus was pulled on a string over the ox, the lake, the shadows in the north woods, the eyes, the holy word—all blue.

I think what happened in history is insignificant to the eye—a man called Jesus and his followers. They didn't seem like much at the time. When Jesus was taken, his disciples fled because they were weak with unbelief. But afterwards they must have seen him again. Whatever Christianity is, it's a kingdom that's invisible unless by need you are born into it, then it's the blue hereafter you see.

Jesus and his group of men had seen another world and gave up everything for it. We could do no less, but marry that reflection of the sky in the map as an image of the world we could not yet see, but was there, delivered by a paltry band of men and a leader who were not much recognized, but came with a message that once you heard and entered, you were never the same again.

It's like we know we are in Christ, but can't know it's true until we get to his house and he unwraps us from himself, and we can't remember the troubles we had on the way.

I prophesy above the glacial plate of the north shore. Come up—O come up with me. It's a unique perception—not seeing as things are, but seeing those things which are not as though they are—Romans 4:17, which are the tenets of faith that can shift things out of their place.

For a while it seemed as though Agoba would crack like the ice that expands and crawls over itself. She grew black eyes on her forehead, those spirit eyes we have inside our head actually showed on her forehead! But it wasn't a transformation of the purest light as it should have been. In the night, Juna called us to feel the feathers on her arms and back. The beak of her mouth just under her nose. I petted Agie until I could see the blue light of the hereafter transformed into something like a loon with circles around the eyes like the sun when you look too close.

The snow is so white, she said, the white so cold it's blue.

# MONKEY TREE

No lions or tigers, no mamma snake. . . .

SONNY AND BROWNIE,
*SAIL AWAY*—

Imagine a world upsidedown—the p is a b, and the b, a p—

Sboon, fork, blate. That's what was on the taple. They said he had disblexia. Words to him were runners. They looked different to him than they did to others. He read what was on the bage, put it was not what others saw. He could not understand what they saw. He could not understand why they didn't see what he saw. He wrote what he saw, and they said it was not what was there. Or what was there, he didn't see.

He was dubed. He was scalded. He was given eyes that did not see things the way they were seen. He came from Toma to the Willatoona school. He could not read. He could not write. The radiator was plasting. It was cold and stormy as the night Puddy Holly went down near Clear Lake just off I-35 south of the Minnesota / Iowa porder.

His father liked Sonny Terry and Prownie McGhee. He listened to their plues—We will cross the mighty ocean into Charleston Pay. It was not the Atlantic coast, put the packwaters of rural America where the sun never hit with its lightness. He wrote a crude sign on a biece of cardpoard and but it on his door—Charleston Pay. That's what he named his blace. He had not crossed the ocean like them, put had peen here since the peginning.

He was in school after school. None turned out anything other than failure. The albhapet was ubsidedown. On its side. Scattered. It changed blaces pefore his eyes. Crashed. The way he sbilled a buzzle to the floor and some of the bieces lay face down, and the buzzle would never go together pecause his buzzle pox didn't have a bicture of what the bieces looked like when they were together.

He stood with his packback in the barking lot waiting for his father. He imagined butting avocados / mangos on the monkey tree. Showing them bieces of his world. Sometimes in reading, he saw Puddy's face at his blane window glittering with ice that will bull him down.

What of these words loaded on a blane too heavy with cold? What of the window that sees what?—the ground coming up?

The storm of misread words licked the blane. He saw ice dancing as it panked into the edge of a storm tearing off his wings and he flew into this new, this bromised world.

# THE ONLY OAR YOU HAVE

An approaching vehicle casted light

"Survival," Arnold Louie

There were rumors going around: Arnie loves Janice

## I. The Church of the Assumption

Janice heard voices in the water. They came across the lake in canoes. She had seen the clouds curled on top like rows of waves coming to the shore. The elders, the grandfathers, paddled the canoes.

"We burn wolf dung for warmth," they said.

On the shore, she listened for their wolf voices. What day was it? When she was a girl, she had lost her coat. Her mother couldn't buy her another one, and she wrapped in a blanket to walk to school. Now it was days she lost. She was with friends. Yes, they had stopped somewhere. Before she knew it, time shifted. It was light again, then dark. Time was like the waves. Some larger, some smaller. The waves were always changing, never the same. Once they came to the shore they tried to turn back, but other waves behind them ran over them.

She saw the image of the moon in the day sky. It was an aluminum paddle broken off its handle. The bottom of the sky was flat against Lake Vermilion. She had to stop drinking. Why did she get drunk over and over? She heard the repetition of the waves. The wind was cold against her face. She pulled a blanket around her head. What if there were as many moons as clouds?

There was a stone church down the road.

"This is how you get into Christianity," the preacher said. He was from the Church of the Assumption on the north shore of

Minnesota, a church based upon the assumption that Christ was, that he had died on the cross, that he had risen. "That truth was a freighter that floated," the preacher said.

Janice Boudreau went to church because she needed Christ as a husband. Marriage had betrayed her. Her husband had left her with three children. She had to have a husband she could not see, feel or taste. Christ, her new husband, was invisible, unseen. Yet he was there with support, like the water that held up ships.

"You reach Christianity with an oar," the preacher said.

Janice was in a place she couldn't row out of. A black cloud swept toward her. She didn't come home several nights. She had two boys and a girl who would want supper. She was guilty of abandoning her children. The welfare agency would take them, but if she tried, she could get them back. If she just made an effort. She got up in the morning and sat at the table. The school bus had come and gone. Her children were still asleep since they'd stayed up later than she had last night. Soon the school would call. She would get them up, drive them to school. They'd be there by lunch. By the time she turned around, they were back.

She didn't want them to come in the door. She drank to prepare for their return. Then she could stumble around the kitchen, fix nothing in particular for supper, grow angry if they complained.

She couldn't sleep without drinking. She couldn't sleep unless she passed out from drinking.

Someone cut down the row of trees along the road—the row the lumber company left. The whole ground shook. She held onto her bed to keep from falling out. Now the land was bare. There was just land and sky, as if the land was a lake. And now there was snow.

It was 10 below. The wind blew thin sheets of snow across the road.

She had stopped at the store for milk and groceries. A car next to her was stalled. Could they use their jumper cables on her car?

While she was in the store they connected her car to theirs and recharged their battery.

When she started down Vermilion Reservation Road, her own car stalled. She sat on the road in the dark. No one came. She got out and walked. The thin strip of sky between the pines in the distance migrated with the stars. They were animal herds on their way across the winter sky: the bear, the wolf, the moose, the fox. The sky was covered with black soot, but the footsteps uncovered the white snow underneath. That's what the stars were. Footsteps of the animals across the sky.

She saw her breath in the frozen air. It was as if she had eaten the moon. Just a few nights ago, the first bites were taken. Finally, only a curve of the top crust was left.

She could fall into the snow and not get up. But she kept walking. She thought of the man killed in the woods when she was a girl. What if she had called out when she heard them in the woods? Would it have kept the other man from killing him? Maybe it was the voice of someone else murdered in the woods. Often the dead left behind their voices behind.

Finally a government car stopped.

"Why're you out in the cold night?"

She had eaten the moon, she told him. The man drove her home—took her in the house and looked at her feet and hands.

"You'll be all right," he said.

He would use his jumper cables on her car. If he got it started, he'd call his back-up and they'd drive the car home. If he couldn't get it started, he'd bring the groceries to her.

"It's just cereal and milk," she told him.

"You shouldn't go out by yourself at night."

"My children are hungry in the morning."

"You should have thought of that earlier."

She would not drink again. The noise of the children would not drive her crazy. She would make them stop fighting. She would find a job. She would live on subsidy and commodities and what she earned and whatever her mother gave her. Sometimes a man stayed for a night, but she didn't see him again. Sometimes the man took their food. He ate before her children could, then he was gone and her children cried from hunger. Her brother-in-law ran off one of the men. Once, her husband, Arnie, showed up, frightening them all. But she wouldn't let him in the door. The spirits must have helped her. He went away without getting in. But she always had to make sure the door was locked and the windows closed. Even when she was so drunk she couldn't get to her bed and lay on the floor, the door was locked and the windows closed.

She would not drink again. But the noise of the children filled her ears. The frustration of her life washed over her. The hopelessness. Helplessness. The grossness. The poverty. Nothing would happened to change her circumstances. It would be the same to the end. She was afraid of the black cloud that sometimes swept over her.

She wanted to lift a bottle to her mouth. She wanted the taste that made her choke. It was a craving. It was power. It numbed. It soothed. It was medicine. It was hope. It didn't last, they told her in counseling. It only made it worse. It was destructive. It was sinister. It made her feel whole while it gutted her. That was drink. She had to have it. She cried for it. When she didn't have money, she begged for it at Crow's, and sometimes the bar tender gave her a bottle with some whiskey in the bottom of it. Sometimes he pushed her out. She cried at her brothers' graves. They were on the other side. They didn't have to live in this world that made mothers drink and forget their children.

"They ought to lock this stuff up," she told the bartender.

"I'd marry this in a minute," another woman said.

"You already have," the bartender answered.

"More addictive than a husband."

"More addictive than a paycheck."

A pine tree caught the clouds passing above it. What day was it?

This was a dream she had over and over.

"She was a girl," they say.

She had bright blue hair parted in the middle and braided into circles and coiled behind her ears. She wore a birch-bark dress. She was sitting on a large buffalo. She sat sidesaddle on its back. The sky behind her was neon yellow. She carried a lizard pocket book.

Soberness would arrive on the shore like a canoe. She would cross the water.

A desire for soberness rowed into her head through her ear. For a moment, it stayed.

Down the road, the stone church sat in a clearing. She rowed toward it. She wanted to go back. To start again. But how could she go to church when the lake was moving? She saw how it angled into the land, spilling onto the shore, which was gray and dim and cold and cut with the cry of gulls and the fog horns of freighters.

Freighters? Yes, she saw them there. Two of them out on the water.

What lake was it? Not Vermilion or Birch Lake. But Superior. Had she taken Highway 1 to the Great Lake? How did she get there? Her friends must have driven. She must have slept for fifty miles.

She wanted to begin again with her young husband, Arnie, her three children, Hunter, Craig, Ewa, when they were still babies—her life when she could handle it. But she had never been able to handle it. They had been doomed from the beginning.

The preacher was not the same preacher who had been in the stone church when she was a girl. There had been several. They all came and went, dazed with disappointment, hardship, and the hopelessness of the reservation. In the front door out the back. It was the hopelessness of the reservation that confronted the church, made of stone that it was, covered with blizzards, and the cries of gulls.

Now she was back in the stone church. Her days moved in and out of one another. Place as well as time was interchangeable.

"There is a shore for you," the preacher said.

She had heard it before but hadn't believed.

"Assume Christianity says what it says it says."

But what does it say? That's the question. It always had confused her, the missionaries arguing over their faith. The one true way to God was littered with many ways. It was pebbles underfoot. She could slip. To many, this God meant nothing. Her friends came to church, and left, and never came again.

No, it wasn't easy. She would feel her body pull her back down. She would have to work against that pull to get up. But she would rise.

"Have you ever stepped into the water?" The preacher asked. "Yes, I can hear you say, straight down through it."

She saw yard lights in the preacher's eyes as he talked. Everywhere else it was dark. This preacher would not go away as easily as the others. But the reservation would wear him down. Just give it time.


She was sedated. The room stayed in one place. Only her eyes moved. Where was she? The Indian Health Clinic. Where had they found her? In the woods near Crow's. She had an ache in her head. She closed her eyes, tried to draw back into the darkness, but the pain followed her. She tried to move, but she was tied down. She struggled, but couldn't move. Her head swam. She felt like she was in a canoe on a choppy lake. It swayed back and forth. She was sick to her stomach, but nothing came up. Now her head pounded. She cried out, but it hurt.

A woman came to her bed.

"You're strapped down so you won't hurt yourself. You would be flying off the walls otherwise. You've had DT's. You're on medication to control them. You're over the worst part."

"I don't remember the worst part."

"That's because of the medication."

"I have a headache." She felt tears in her eyes. Her head pounded again and she winced.

"I'll get you something," the woman said. "You were beaten. Do you remember?"

She shook her head, no.

"You've got stitches above your eyes."

Two of her sisters were there then. She was awake again. Even the youngest who had gone to the university on a scholarship and married into a white family and lived in the city. She came back to see the squalor her oldest sister lived in. She was there with her girl, probably ten or eleven. Janice squinted to see her. The girl had a horrified look on her face. She knew how she looked because of the girl's face. Why did her youngest sister bring her? Did she want her daughter to see what not to do? Did she want to scare the girl out of drinking? This would be the easiest way. Show her Aunt Janice. Show her what a beat-up face looked like, arms tied to the bed. Mouth caked with crust.

## II. The Moon on Their Breath

"She was a girl," they say.

It had been autumn and her feet made noises in the leaves. Somewhere a truck turned off the highway and bounced in the ruts of the dirt road. She could hear the tools rattle in the truckbed from the distance. The reservation houses had been built on an old logging road. Under the dirt, a bed of logs lay crosswise under the road. She felt the wind blow strands of hair across her face. The wind in the trees sounded like water in a shallow stream. It sounded like pencils writing in school.

The land was flat. Pines, birch and tamaracks had lined up against the road. The reservation was on a moraine. There had been spirits in the old glacier and the spirits had grown hair for warmth. When the glacier melted, the spirits shed their hair, and their hair became the trees.

Down the road, a stone church sat in another clearing. There were a few trailers and mailboxes along the main road.

The girl bent forward to make her way into the clump of brush where she played in the summer. She came into the woods to get away from her house; her two brothers and three younger sisters. She had a doll, which was her friend, more than a dependent. Someday she would have children. She knew it. There was nothing else for her to want. In the woods she made a bed of pine needles. She used twigs for pillows. The clump of brush was shaped like a beaver mound. She thought of the old story of beavers, how they once had been big as buffalo, but their dams flooded the country. The Great Spirit had to rework his plan for the beaver, make them smaller. The brush clump moved with flickering sun and shadows. In places, flat slabs of granite sat on the ground, covered with moss and lichen. Once she tried to get some moss from the woods to grow by her house, but it died.

The truck she had heard stopped, or it was another truck. She heard a car also. Two men came into the woods. They had words. She hid in the clump of brush. The men were fighting louder now. She heard a thunk, a groan, a heavy thud. One man fell. There were footsteps running through the leaves. The car starting. Driving off.

Now the girl heard a car on the road and she walked along the edge of a yard until it passed. All the houses on Vermilion Reservation Road had a gravel drive to a clapboard or shingled house, or a trailer. Several cars, few of which would start, sat in the yards. She couldn't remember if her mother or grandmother knew where she went. Often they didn't know where her two brothers and three sisters were, once they were old enough to leave the house.

The dead man was from somewhere else. There were rumors and questions. She had left her doll in the woods, and they brought it to her. She told the authorities she hadn't seen anything. She had heard the scuffle, but she didn't know what it was about. That's how it was. There were strange happenings on the reservation. People disappeared. People were found dead of no apparent cause. She remembered her strange dreams. Everything was lifted out of order. Years were interchangeable. Events shuffled. They knew it too. How was she supposed to know what happened? Her brothers fought in the other room. Her sisters were crying. The authorities left her mother's small house.

Sometimes she thought she heard the men in the woods again in the night, but maybe it was a dream. She thought of her doll dressed in buckskin with its blank face.


She was older now and a boy, Arnie Boudreau, in the next grade, stood on the road ahead of her. He asked her to a dance. Her mother wouldn't care, but she said she'd have to ask her.

"Have you asked?" He found her at school.

"No," she said.

The next day he asked again.

"Yes, she said I could," she said.

Janice had worn an ordinary dress, and he held her. She had felt him against her. She had gone to another dance and another. He put his cigarette into her mouth and gave her some of his beer.

She had gone to the stone church when she was a girl.

Blessed be the cold for in it we huddle together.

Blessed be the weather from the north—Job 37:22.

Blessed be the storehouses of hail—Job 38:22.

Blessed be the winter.

What kind of God lived in a country where blessed weather came from the north? She wanted to ask. But the Sunday school teacher didn't like questions.

Janice had sat beside her grandmother in church. When her grandmother died, she didn't go to church.


The boy in the next grade was no longer in school. He had an old black car with an Indian blanket over the seat. He stormed the reservation roads. There was no work for him anywhere. One door shut on him and another. He waited for her in the parking lot at school. Sometimes he pulled her away before she went into the building. Sometimes he waited after school. The trees flopped their wings when the car passed. When he had been beat down hard enough, he cried against her shoulder. Later in the winter, she married him.

Blessed be the ice, for by it the breadth of waters is narrowed—Job 37:10.

Then Janice and Arnie had children—Hunter, Craig and Ewa. The doll was far back in her drawer. They tried to move to the city but the city pushed them back. For a while they lived with her husband's relatives but the relatives got tired of them.

There was a tract house near her mother with a gravel drive and a yard filled with old cars and junk. No one had lived there for a year. She moved into the house. Sometimes after that, Arnie left. Neighbors helped her put glass in the boarded-up windows and take the junk from the yard. Her mother watched the children while she worked.

Sometimes, walking with her children near the woods, she remembered the brush clump where she had played. She remembered a man had been killed. By then, her husband didn't come home from work.

Blessed be the men not fit to sleep with dogs—Job 30:1.

Blessed be the men who roam the desolate land—Job 30:3.

Blessed be those who are driven away—Job 30:5.

Janice often thought of Arnie with an ache. The reservation was even harder on the men than it was the women, and it was hard on the women.

But by then, she didn't want him to come back. He was angry and frustrated and could not keep his hurt to himself. He had raged at them for making him responsible. He hated the family for giving him a job he couldn't do: being able to provide. The children wanted bicycles. They wanted video games. He pushed them out of his sight. They stayed in the woods when he came home. She showed the children where she'd played as a girl. She showed them how to make an opening in a clump of brush where they hid during the night. In winter they went to the shelter. The welfare agency came and said he had to leave. He couldn't stay with his family. He left and she knew sometimes in the night he drove by the house. She knew when he stood at the back door. She could hear the gravel under the car in the drive. She knew the spirits protected her. She heard them in the yard. The roots of trees still reached into the earth, though the trees had been cut into lumber to make wood for houses, and pulp for the paper mill. The logging company took the trees and left a margin along the roads as if the land was still full. But she could look into the trees beside the road and see the land was vacant. Another glacier would have to cover the land again. And the hair of the spirits caught in the ice and became trees when the glacier melted.

Now her husband was gone and no one knew where he was. Maybe he had been killed. Maybe the spirits had taken him so he wouldn't hurt the children. Maybe he left Minnesota and went somewhere to start another family. Maybe he was neglecting them. Maybe he was beating them now.

She woke in the night with sweat. What would she do? How would she raise the children? How would she buy them winter coats? How long would the food stamps last? She had used most of them and the rest of the month was ahead. There was a food shelf in the stone church. She would say her "blessed bees" and go. There were hoards of them buzzing her heels. The church was a hive.

Now the children's fighting and sicknesses got her down and she could not get up. She had more than she could do. She knew the struggle her husband had faced and the anger raised up in her. If only he would come back, she thought at times, but put the thought away. Blessed be the husband who does not come back. What if she never knew what happened to him? She was blessed. She could hear the houses where husbands raged and the wives screamed back. Why didn't the spirits take those men too? She could hear the cars of the welfare agency.

She saw men she knew with younger women now while their wives and children waited at home. After so many years, she could claim her husband was legally dead. But who would want her with three children to raise and a face that had started to sag? One day she found her old doll in a box and cried.

Her grandmother would have known what plants to use from the woods. She would have known how to heal her. Her mother didn't seem to know. She was only full of superstition.

There had been old secrets, but they had been kept so secret they were gone. The church worked to make its secrets known. There were sermons anyone could hear. How strange it had seemed at first. She liked the magic parts of the Bible where an angel folded itself into a flame and went up to heaven—Judges 13:20. Sometimes she wanted to go up to heaven too.

When her boys played with matches in the woods and started a brush fire, she imagined the smoke was an angel rising into the sky. The firemen put out the fire and the reservation authorities told her to watch her children.

The pines and birch and tamaracks moaned in the air with the blizzard. She sat in the stone church looking at a hymn book in the rack on the pew in front of her. She saw the two altar candles in the distance as if they were headlights coming toward her.

She stayed after church for the dinner. She could hear her children fighting downstairs. They sounded like loons. She went to the church basement and tried to stop them. What didn't they understand? She was pleading with them in front of others. She was stifling her anger. They were in church to hear God and to eat food. They had to behave or be sent away hungry.

After church she went to Crow's while her children played with friends. Her own friends were there, drinking, talking, playing pool. They played pull tabs. They played video games. They went home with one another.

The room was distorted again. A neighbor and her mother brought some medicine. Both women were so old she thought they were spirits. They held up her head up and she drank the tea they gave her. She choked on it and they waited until she stopped. She asked them to get her doll out of the drawer. The doll carried the woods with her. The doll carried the bend of light and shadow across the branches of the brush clump. The doll carried the memory of a man's death with her. The doll carried the light jumping in the breeze. In the dark, she could see the light coming from the doll.

She remembered being in school under the gray sky dull as pencil lead. Why had she let it pass? Why had she given away the opportunity? Her youngest sister had taken it and now lived in the city.

Where had her old Sunday School teacher gone? Maybe the Great Spirit had taken her up in a flame.

In the beginning there was winter. The Great Spirit set his animals in the snow to mark their footprints, hoof prints, paw prints.

There was something she liked about church. She could think of her own stories there. She could mix them with Bible stories. The world of men always would be clamped with self-interest, greed, the acts of the stronger over the weaker. But what about the world of God? Didn't he subsume the weak also? Wasn't it the lost that Jesus sought? She saw the small, round communion wafers. They were like paw prints on the plate. What was it she heard from the minister during communion at the stone Church of the Assumption? The minister said she was supposed to die to herself and live for God. She had to let his will overtake hers. *They were eating Christ*, the minister said. But wasn't Christ eating her? Wasn't she Christ's communion wafer? Wasn't it the other way around?

## III. When the Language Parted

Now the birds were fussing.

They were pouring a story into her ear. Someone else was there. Talking to her and talking. They were telling her of soberness. It was something that she wanted to hold.

She had had two brothers and three sisters. One brother had been killed in a car accident. The other shot himself while hunting when he was eleven. She thought of them sometimes. Once, the older one appeared in a dream. She wondered if her own two boys carried the spirits of her brothers. It made her cry to think of them. She drank to numb the pain.

Her boys did not act like spirits. They fought in the house. They fought in the yard. They fought in school and she had to go get them because the teachers didn't know what to do with them.

How many dependents do you have? When was the last time you looked for a job? Do you have problems with alcohol?

Sometimes when she drank, her mother stayed at the house with her children. When her mother could not handle them, or had too many children because her younger sister had brought her children to her, the welfare agency came and got them.

"You're not taking them," Janice cried. She tried to stop them from leaving, but she fell on the porch. She passed out before the welfare agency car disappeared from sight.

She would not drink again. She could do better, her mother said. She was a mother now too, that should be enough.

But it wasn't. Why didn't she understand what it was like? Her children were not enough. Her children were eating her.

Somewhere the crows squawked, answering one another with loud caws. In the noise of birds, she heard the ghosts of old tribes. Their skirmishes spoke through the damp, cold trees. Now it was her brothers. The sisters she heard.

There were heavy clouds over Lake Vermilion. The roads: Vermilion Reservation Road, Whiskey Point, Boise Forte, Cemetery Road, Duffy Point, Gruban Road, Manitou Road, West Two Road off Highway 1. The Vermilion Reservation was at the end of the Vermilion Trail, once an old Indian path from Duluth to Pike Bay on Lake Vermilion. The land was full of lakes and sloughs; the

Mesaba soil, the dark mix of blue and redbrown. Trees against the road.

She had drawn trees with purple trunks and reddish, blue-brown leaves. The woods had spoken to her when she was a girl. Her doll had told her what the leaves said. In the winter, the doll talked to her about the snow. She still could hear its voice.

## i) The brother who shot himself hunting

We was walking near the slough. Saw a rabbit. Running after him. Tripped. The finger in the trigger pulled. Shot right through my jaw. I was walking there. I know I was. I heard a spirit from heaven say, "um wake. Bring him. He needin." I saw the spirit make a zero in the slough. I was still alive and my brother and the others fighting. I felt the blood running out. I thought I could pull the blood back into my wound. Put a finger on the vein. It was pumping out my life.

Sometimes if Janice dozed she could hear the shot. She could feel him near the slough. She didn't want to go there. When Arnie wanted to park, she refused to stop there.

## ii) The brother who died in car accident

The car hit the railroad track

############################################

Burst off the road. Bompt! Wheeled around. Rolled. Stomped a tree. It was quiet. An animal howled. The others in the car stopped calling. The broken bone was sticking out of my back. A girl was crying. Was it spirits coming around to take us? We lifted up. We walked. Look! The car in pieces just like bones. Skid marks 100 yards. It was a moose in the road, he said, made us hit them tracks. No, he always had an excuse. The moose was off to the side still frozen in the one car light.

### iii) The sister who died

My hands fly like birds. I can't hold them still.


### iv) The sister talking about her mother

She wore out. There was no one to help her. Her husband was dead. Her sisters and brothers gone. They pulled her with them like an old canoe on a tow line.


## IV. Sober

Everything was out of proportion. Larger than it should have been.
 That's what it was like to be sober.
 A beaver building a dam flooding the country.
 If she tried to stay sober, she was shunned. There was no room on the reservation for soberness. But even if no one would go with her, she would row.
 Her friends stayed by the lake drinking. She longed to be with them. She tried to go to church, but Christianity was a lonely religion, just she and Christ. It was lonely as soberness, which was the moon by itself in the night sky. It was a loon call in the dark.


This is what it felt like to be sober: everything she didn't want to be, everything she wasn't. She held out her tongue to the night. She could see the moon's breath coming from her mouth.
 She could see the wreck of her life. Nothing would draw it back together. Somewhere her father died.
 Somewhere her mother died.
 There were wakes and funerals and she didn't know where she was. They held her up. Who? Arnie? No, it couldn't be him. She was dreaming. Her husband had vanished long ago. She couldn't remember him. Maybe it was someone who looked like him. She remembered looking at his face. Staring until they laughed at

her. She couldn't focus. She couldn't get it straight. Time swirled around her.

Somewhere one of her sisters died, not the youngest one in the city, but another one, like her.

She was at another wake. Another funeral. She couldn't tell them apart, but tossed with the waves on the lake.

Her old doll was eating her. If she stayed in her room, she heard the drawer open. She felt the doll climb on the bed. Sometimes she let the doll nibble her fingers. It didn't hurt. She let the doll eat one arm. One leg.

"She was a girl," they say, but they were talking about the doll.

The preacher had an aluminum paddle. He rowed. The doll rowed. Now she was the canoe they rowed. Now the moon was a canoe she rowed. Everything was water.

This is what it was like to be sober: everything running together. The moon torn in half. One side of it thrown away. The remaining half longing for the other.

She remembered the sparkle of old glass bottles by Lake Vermilion. Buttons. Coins. Clay marbles. She could dig along the lake shore and find pieces of old pottery. Sometimes archeologists from the Minnesota Historical Society bought them.

Lake Vermilion was red in the dusk.

Firewater. Rainwater. Moonwater. Lakewater. Holywater. She called drinking all of these. She wanted it and wanted it. It didn't go away.

The preacher let her stay in the stone church at night. She lay on the floor and held the table legs. She licked the stone floor.

That was what it was like to be sober.

She had one boy, Hunter, in the reformatory. Her daughter, Ewa, and baby were living with a boy and his sister who also had a baby. She couldn't ask how they were. She couldn't bear her weight and theirs too. Her other son, Craig, in the army in a war in Iraq somewhere. Or was it Afghanistan?

She heard the spirits. They rode snowmobiles of the purest light. The cold air came from their mouths and noses. Their eyes were snow-dogs—the sun through frozen air. She drove to Birch Lake where Highway 1 narrowed through the birch forest. The trees were tall, ghostly and white. They were full of eyes. The spirits lived there—"I speak to you from a world you don't know." It was a sober world. A holy world which had drunkenness for its counterfeit.

She heard the voices of the trees.

Blessed be the birch.

She called to her friends. Most everyone was drunk still floating in the water. There is nothing on shore, they said. She called to them, come, oh come. He is merciful and forgiving. He is the only oar you have. He is transforming.

The only oar you have is.

## V. Voices

Her daughter, Ewa, was drinking now. The boys came for her.

She left the baby with anyone. It was a strange baby with large dark eyes and hairs that stuck up on its head like whiskers. Sometimes her daughter left it alone. Janice asked her daughter to bring the baby to her house. Once Janice drove to her daughter's boyfriend's sister's house and took the baby to hide it from the welfare agency. It was two days before her daughter called crying she couldn't find her baby.

"I'm hiding her until you get straightened out," Janice said.

"I want her back," Ewa said.

"The welfare agency will take her," she said. "You can visit her. You can stay with me if you want."

But her daughter didn't want to stay with her, and left.

Janice carried the baby around the house during the day. It had trouble sleeping. It cried. She rocked it and rocked it. Where did she get the patience? In the old days, she'd be out the door, as her daughter was now.

She saw her daughter in places she didn't want to see her. She saw her coming out of Crow's with the boyfriend's father. The daughter was living the life her mother had.

The daughter came back pregnant again.

"Who's the father this time?"

Her daughter wouldn't tell her.

There were pills Ewa could take that would make her sick if she drank. Janice had taken them before. She might need them again. She knew where she could get them. The Indian Health Clinic.

The baby howled. Janice rocked it. Sometimes she let it cry. Sometimes she walked to the backyard and sat by herself as she listened to the baby, hoping it would fall asleep. It had to get into the groove of sleep.

The medicine man came and burned cedar. He called a cloud over the child's head. He tried to straighten the baby's crooked little cry. The women from the church prayed. One of the women from the church took the baby one morning to give her a rest from its crying.

The doctor at the Indian Health Clinic changed its formula.

She got her old doll out of the drawer. She put the doll in the baby's bed. It was still dressed in his buckskin dress, with a bead hanging loose on a thread, which she pulled off.

Maybe the old light would come from the doll.

No, it was the voices the baby needed. She was crying from of the desolation she heard. The silenced stories. The baby needed to be surrounded by the old ones, their stories, their breath. The separation was beyond endurance, and the baby broke.

She told it stories. Ones she could remember. How huge beavers had to be remade. But that was all she remembered and silence stopped her voice. Blessed be the groaning of the earth— Romans 8:22.

Blessed be the groaning that cannot be uttered—Roman 8:26.

She started another story for the baby. It was a story about the trees. But she grew quiet again. How could she tell her the lumber company cleared the land?

There he was all of a sudden, the old husband, Arnie, looking at her. For some reason, she thought of a walrus, the one who walks with his teeth. Or a moose. Or the old moss from the woods she had tried to grow once when she was a girl.

"I told the spirits to tell you I was coming," he said.

"I didn't hear them."

"It's a rough life."

"You know, you haven't been around long enough. You don't remember the children you've got and now the grandchild."

"I been here more than you know," Arnie said. He looked at the baby. It was nothing to him.

"I'm surprised you're still alive," she said.

"I got a disease that's killing me."

"Craig's overseas. Hunt's in the reformatory," she told him.

"I seen Hunt. He's getting out."

"He can come back here as long as he doesn't drink and finds a job."

"You asking him to do what you can't."

"That's probably right," she said, "except I got a job. The welfare agency hired me. I raised the children without you."

"That's the way it is," he said, "although it shouldn't have to be."

"Where you been?" Janice asked.

"In the cities," Arnie answered.

"You been married?"

"Yes."

"You married now?" She asked.

"No."

"You always talked about leaving. Going somewhere else—"

"I did. Nothing there."

"Why're you back?"

"I remembered the bed of logs under the road. When dirt gets washed out in the spring, the car rattles over the road. Some things you don't forget."

"A jittering car brought you back?"

"Where you going now?" He asked.

"I got washing to do. I put the baby on the machine. It's where she can sleep."

The land was flat, except for a few slopes. There were tamaracks, birch and pines across the moraine of northern Minnesota. Trailers. Mailboxes. She was on her way to the stone church through the night dampness of Vermilion Reservation Road. The church was where she and the children had gotten food when there was no place else. The church was where the welfare agency let her hold sessions with recovering alcoholics who were women. The same preacher was still there, the one she thought would leave, the one she thought would wash away.

She rocked the baby and listened to the voices of the women in the alcoholic meeting at the stone church. The baby with the round eyes and stubble on its head listened too.

### i) Someone built a fire to boil water.

Or it could have started in a trailer up the road. Maybe someone camping in the woods. Their bodies roasted. Their arms lifted like branches left on a tree.

### ii) There's never nothin I do.

I drift back up to Crow's at night. Then afternoon. My friend don't want to drink but I keep pushin' it on 'er. Otherwise them dogs come 'round. They bark at the door. I see their eyes on the ceiling at night. I can't hold a glass unless I'm drinkin'.

## iii) I dreamed I had a horse named, Jasper.

A large horse with a long neck. I rode ride him around the pasture, his mane flapping against my hands as I held the reins and saddle horn. I kept him in a paddock with an open shed. On nights below zero I put his horse blanket on. I asked the spirits to blow their breath on him for warmth. He had a mark on his haunch. He snorted a cloud of breath from his nose. I gave him grain. He let some of it fall for the mice who sleep in the bales of hay. Jasper's neck grew longer. I was afraid he would trip. I rode him in the cold. My breath was the same as his. I saw the mark on his haunch was a frozen lake. His long legs were inlets. I heard the cry of a loon. I found he was a boat, his neck the only oar I had.

Janice fed the baby and rocked her before dawn. She could hear the other voices as she rocked.

There had been six children in her family. The two boys were dead. One sister had died. The other two were still alive. The middle sister had numerous children, including some of the dead sister's. The youngest sister had made it away from the reservation. She had gone to school. Was that it? Was that how she got out of the destruction that held everyone in its wake?

Her parents were dead also. She couldn't remember when her father had died. He had been in and out of her life like the clouds she saw speed by.

Her mother had died when Janice was drunk, and she couldn't remember when she had died. It was in a fog. It even seemed at times she was still alive.

On days the baby could not stop crying, Janice drove her to Lake Vermilion so she could hear the voices in the water. The ripple of the loons.

The ones who had been there left their voices. They canoe the water. They rift the waves. How do you make your way? You don't drink. But the afternoon gets thirsty. The nights more. You drink

THE ONLY OAR YOU HAVE

to hear the old ones row the water. You drink to tell them you can hear. The lake spreads under the sky.

Whisper the wind in two.

Fork it like an upstream river.


Janice had a call from the Indian Health Clinic. They had a woman from her group with DT's. The woman was seeing dogs. She was tied to the bed. She thrashed until she nearly broke the cords. They gave her further medication.

Janice sat with the woman. She told the woman she had a stick. She was beating away the dogs.

Blessed be the dogs that compass me—Psalm 22:16.


She was peeling an onion for the supper stew.

She was supposed to dice it, but she kept peeling sheet after curved sheet. The outside layers were thin and transparent as waxed paper. Inside, the onion was damp and shiny as the white tip of a loon feather. She began to put the layers together again. She had a rubberband in the drawer. She could hold it together with that. She had the sting of onion in her eyes, on her hands. She made a wad of rumpled onion. It was torn and ragged as the earth she held.

Janice froze in the chair after supper. It was Hunter, her son. She hadn't seen him in several months. He came as a ghost of himself. She wanted to cry, but she got up from the chair. There was a scar across his forehead. He'd been in a knife fight in the reformatory. He winced when she touched his arm. There were more stitched there.

"You're letting the world tear you up."

She saw him shiver on the sofa and covered him with a blanket though it was summer. He let out a noise that was something like a sob muffled by a cough.

"Your sister's pregnant by her boyfriend's father. She won't admit it. But I can tell when I see him. The boyfriend's going to find out about it and beat her. She's not 20 and soon the mother of two children. I can't do anything to help her, but maybe it's not too late for the baby. If she gets a few good years."

Janice went to the backyard. A cloud of mosquitoes quilted her.


Hunter and her old husband, Arnie, slept in the room Hunter and Craig, his younger brother, had shared. Maybe Craig would come back too.

They would take as many fish from Vermilion as they wanted. Their ancestors had fished the lake. It was their land.

If she could get her children in school. They could go to Duluth. There was aid for Indian students. She talked to them about the University of Minnesota at Duluth, but they were not interested. They could live off the land. They could live off welfare. Off dealing in the casinos. Off girlfriends.

She worked for the welfare agency. She answered calls. She worked from her house. She could take care of the baby and let the welfare agency know where they were needed. She knew the reservation. She could decipher the calls. Relay the messages. Tell the agency what she thought the problem was.

Her old husband laughed. "You used to run from them now they've got you working for them."

"I'm working for the people."

"Sure you are."

"You remember they came after you," she told him. "They saved me from you."


Janice came back tired from church late at night. There had been weeping at the women's session. A woman who came drunk had to be removed. The preacher could not lift her off the floor, but called the reservation authorities who took her to the Indian Health Clinic.

Janice put the baby in its bed when she got back.

The next morning she woke late. She knew it as she woke. It was not before dawn. It was mid-morning. How could she have slept? Did Arnie or Hunter feed the baby?

Everyone was gone.

Had they fed the baby and put her back to sleep?

She looked in the crib. The baby was gone. Arnie was gone, but she found Hunter still asleep. She woke him.

"Where's the baby?"

He didn't know.

She drove down reservation roads: Whiskey Point, Boise Forte, Duffy Point, Gruban Road, Manitou.

She called the authorities, but didn't know what to say. She could tell them to find Arnie, but he wouldn't take the baby. She reported the baby missing and hung up.

Where was her daughter living now? She drove to the boy-friend's sister's, but the baby wasn't there.

"Where's your father?" Janice asked.

"It isn't him," the boyfriend's sister said. "They ain't together anymore," she said in spite. She called Janice names as she backed from the yard.

Janice decided to call the welfare agency on her daughter.

The next day the welfare agency called. They had her daughter and baby at the Indian Health Clinic. The baby was crying. She could hear her as she started down the hall. She rocked the baby. It grew quiet.

Ewa, her daughter, had taken her baby. She wanted care for it in the run-down place she rented. But the baby cried. She got drunk to drown its cries.

Janice held her daughter, Ewa, rocking her and rocking her. The knot on her wrist? Was it broken?

"Your jaw is swollen. But there's no bruise. Your drinking goes right to the baby," she said to her pregnant daughter. "Would you give your other baby beer to drink all day?"

"My head is full of lard," the daughter said.

"This is the same clinic I was in. Just like you. My sisters came and stared at me. I knew I wanted out."

She rocked her and tried to tell her a story, but the daughter pushed her away.

"I don't want to hear them stories."

"The stories can help you get out."

But they keep the daughter in the clinic. Tied her to the bed or she would leave and drink again.

The daughter cursed her mother, but she would not sign her out.

The medicine man came for a healing ceremony, but Ewa pushed him away.

"You'll have to live with me if you leave the clinic. You can't hold two babies."

Her daughter turned to the wall. "You got Hunter and my father," her daughter said.

"Your father is passing through. Have you known him to stay?"

"He's too sick to go far."

He continued to get worse. She heard him groan in the night. Hunter and the baby could sleep through it. She moved Arnie into the larder off the kitchen where she had a cot for him.

Ewa was staying with her by then too.

Arnie cried for the hurt of the world.

He cried for this wounded earth.

This Indian boarding school.


It was winter again and the geese migrated. The raccoons got into the larder. The loons choked. Once in a while there was a letter from Craig.

There was a splinter in her finger which festered. There was a tree in her eyes which housed birds. There was a rage to drink. Janice held to her chair. She paced. She wanted to sew her head shut. She got in her car and drove until she ran out of gas. She sat in the dark hitting her head against the steering wheel.

She talked to the women in the alcoholic meetings. She had a stone from the lake she handed to the woman beside her. The woman talked and handed the stone to the next woman. The woman would tell her story, and pass the stone. Christ sat with them. They couldn't see him, but he would strengthen them.

The women had missing teeth. They had scarred faces, welts. One was blind in one eye.

"Drinking turns you to bones. It strikes you with lightning," Janice said. She brought the baby to the stone church. She couldn't leave her at home. The baby crawled to the women, sat on their lap. The baby was the stone they passed around. She was the island toward which they rowed.

## VI. The Only Oar You Have

A lament akin to Old Norse, lomr, or loon,
to mourn aloud, to wait, to cry in grief

WEBSTER'S *NEW COLLEGIATE DICTIONARY*

Each journey is a boat over water.

Her old husband lay in a drugged stupor in his bed at the Indian Health Clinic. He knew she was there. He asked for her when she wasn't. Forgiveness was another journey over an open body of water. But it was water she couldn't cross. She had no boat for it. Their land had separated. She was one shore. He was another. They would not join again. He had pulled her down from the beginning, had held his leg out to trip her, had made her stumble, and she had let him.

She knew he had been told he lived in a world in which he didn't belong. She remembered the teachers who made that clear. She knew her brothers heard it, and her sons. They had been ridiculed, beat up, shamed. That was what caused the damage. Shame. For a moment she broke. But it was not love returning. Love was beyond them. What she felt was an understanding, and if not an understanding, it was a recognition of the world he had been pushed into, or had been pushed on him, and if not that, it was an insight into a man who had been her husband, and who was now in a distant land, unreachable. But once in a while, there was a glint of light reflected from something, a broken piece of metal, a pocket knife blade, a moving car on a far island.

She could walk where he couldn't. She could leave the clinic. It was the same clinic where she had been when she was sick with alcoholism. Which room? She walked down one hall, then another. But she couldn't remember the room. She didn't want to know where it was anyway.

When she returned to her house on the Vermilion Reservation Road, she saw a few cars stopped. Why were people standing on the edge of the road? They could be killed that way. There was no accident she could see.

She slowed as she passed the row of cars. There by the woods, she saw what they were watching. A small bear sat against a tree nursing her two cubs. They were probably her first. She knew the cars stopped to watch her. She wanted to show her cubs. The snow had melted. It was cold and raw, but people stayed in their cars with the windows down, or got out and stood by the road. The little mother knew she was acknowledged.


Hunter's car was gone one night when Janice got home. The baby and her daughter were gone. Soon Hunter called from the Indian Health Clinic. The daughter was going to have her baby.

She had just been there. Did they pass on the road without seeing one another?

She returned to the clinic. She sat with her daughter in labor. Hunter held the baby in the waiting room.

"Do you want me to call the father?"

"He wouldn't come."

The daughter's labor was difficult and long. Sometimes Janice had to leave the room. She had eaten sorrow and disappointment, hunger and frustration. She broke apart.

She sat by her old husband's bed.

She returned to her daughter.

"Awaaayaaaa," the daughter cried.

She told Hunter to take the baby home.

She returned to her husband's bed.

She returned to her daughter.

The baby was born toward morning. It looked like it was wearing armor. She sighed with her head against the glass. The armor was something the baby would need.


She sat by her old husband's bed one evening when the preacher came to visit him. Her husband had come out of his stupor. Maybe it was a change in his medication.

"Do you know Christ as your savior?" The preacher asked.

"It was in the mission," Arnie answered. "I had to listen to sermons before I ate. I caught the stone that was thrown out."

"What stone was that?" Janice asked.

"Christ."

She looked at the preacher.

"But it was too late," Arnie continued. "I was sick. I had thrown away my life."

"You're the stone he caught," the preacher said.

"You were my husband," Janice said. "You moved on. I stayed with the children. I can look at you and say where have you been? How could you throw us away? Leave us behind? Did you ever think about us? I'm angry we needed you and you weren't here. Do you know what it feels like to be abandoned?"

He shook his head he did.

"I was in school until you tripped me. You fathered three children and left."

The preacher tried to step in, but she held him back.

"Remember the chair you threw across the room and broke against the wall? That was the first wood I used for kindling. You could have stayed to break up more furniture when we were cold."

"I left before I knocked you across the room."

Their marriage had dropped out of God's heaven and hit water. It had been a fishing boat with a small motor they drove straight into the shore.

The preacher's counseling session wasn't going well. He had to get her out.

"I'd still carve our names in a tree," he told her. "Arnie and Janice." He reached for her, but she backed away.

"The trees have been cut down."

"There's some of them left."

"I can't go back to that bloated island," she told him.

"Sometimes we lose track of ourselves for a while," he said.

"If you could leave us, Janice—" the preacher said.

Sometimes there was a spirit standing in the woods. Sometimes the suddenness of it scared her. But she walked past, or drove past, looking at it with acknowledgment. She knew it was there. It knew she knew it was there, covered with red loon eyes and crying with grief until the cries sounded like laughter.

Christ propped the sky open with his spear and Arnie stepped through.

The Indian Health Clinic called her at dawn. She had not been with him. No one had.

He had seemed better—but then—

She drove to the clinic that morning. She didn't have any clothes to take. He could be buried in his old shirt and trousers.

They stood under the gray sky in the cemetery. Janice knew she was surrounded by her grandmother, mother, sister, friends, her two brothers, father, all of them dead. She also was surrounded by the living ones, diminished by the world they lived in, Hunter, Craig, Ewa. Maybe the two granddaughters still had a chance.

The anger ate her.

She listened to the preacher speak about their gaudy attempts at endurance—their clumsy efforts, which, in Christ, were something akin to dignity.

When she wanted to drift off, the babies pulled her back.

"She was a girl," they say. Janice held the older baby in the yard, and told her stories. "You are sitting on a large buffalo," she said to the baby. "Your hair is braided into circles and coiled behind your ears. The sky is yellow as neon." The older baby sat on her lap as she listened. The baby held an old lizard pocket-book she carried.

Ewa had come in late the night before and was still groggy. She came to the yard carrying the younger baby.

"If I see the father of that baby around here, I'll pray the spirit I saw standing in the woods stands in his way."

"I get lonely."

"Your babies are an island in the water."

"You didn't seem to think so," her daughter remembered.

She woke each dawn with the sound of babies. She changed them, fed them, dressed them. Sometimes Ewa helped. Other times she slept. It was that or drive Ewa away. What did she have anyway? What any old woman had. Children and grandchildren who could not get along on their own.

The land was white and gray and white again. The sky at sundown had a fluorescent haze to it, like the rooms in the Indian Health Clinic. She smelled smoke rising from wood-burning stoves. Always the smell of smoke. Of pines. Of cold. Always the smell of hurt. Hunger. Struggle. Death. It was a hunger that supper could not stop, no matter how many you ate. Sometimes drinking could numb the hunger. That's why Crow's was never vacant. That's why she had been pulled there as if it were a restaurant serving not stew or venison, but whiskey, beer, peanuts, jerky. That's what some of them lived on.

She told the women in the alcoholic sessions to come to her house when they felt driven to Crow's.

"What do you do when you don't go to Crow's."

"You sit in your head with the lights out," she answered. "You die a little. But it's a death that brings you back to life," she explained.

Was it Arnold she remembered? She woke thinking of a red plaid flannel shirt and jeans rolled up. Yes, she remembered the cuffs. Was it him standing in the road, waiting for her?

Sometimes the women from the alcoholic sessions at the stone church slept on her couch or on the cot in the larder. Sometimes they got sick or had dreams that made them scream. The babies didn't seem to mind. They needed the screams to remember where they were. Still on earth. Still alive.

"Why do we have these women in this house?" Ewa was irritated.

What else did she have to do but take care of them who needed her? The desire to help was an open lake within her. Her ability to help was what she could do with the oar she had. In reaching others, she somehow reached herself.

A storm came across the lake. It blew through the trees with a howl. Aiiii. It would have been a blizzard if it were winter. But it was spring. She pulled Ewa and the babies under the kitchen table. The tract house sat flat on the ground. There was nowhere to go. The wind crashed through trees across the road. She was afraid the wind would tear through the house, rip it up by the roots. She sang a song to the storm. Her words were stiff—"Pass over us. Pass above us. Do not rake this house." The wind blew and spit and hissed and bumped against the house. The land rocked back and forth, but the tract house was not blown away.

She could see the younger baby that Ewa held, the one who looked like it wore armor. It stared straight at her, not afraid. She watched the little black apples of its eyes.

"I feel I'm in a boat." Ewa said, holding the baby.

The baby seemed to smile as she glared.

# MALCHAS

Then Simon Peter, having a sword, drew it, and struck the high priest's servant, cutting off his right ear. The servant's name was Malchas.

—JOHN 18:10

One of them smote the servant of the high priest and cut off his right ear. And Jesus said, Permit me, and he touched his ear and healed him.

—LUKE 22:50–51

I remember holding my ear to my head. The doctor tried to sew it on, but there was not enough ear. In time, I would have a prosthetic ear. *Pinna*—the doctor called it—the ear flap outside the head. But the doctor could not replace the other words I learned—ear drum, canal, hammer, stirrup, anvil—

I was with my cousins and other boys lighting fireworks—my father and uncle in the house playing pinochle. No one knew where the bottle-rocket came from. It tipped or fluked and slammed into my head. Then I was underwater somewhere. The sounds I heard were subterranean. The other boys ran. One of the cousins stayed with me until my father and uncle came, my uncle in his under-shirt and suspenders holding up his trousers. I was beached on earth. My mother's screams were piercing. All I could think was that I felt surrounded by the absence of water.

The world came on a gurney. The bright, round light in the surgery-room was the moon. In my head, I carried the explosion of the sun.

My name wasn't Malchas, but they called me that after Miss Pinkney told the Sunday-school class about Malchas—the man whose ear Peter cut off when the soldiers arrested Jesus. But Jesus didn't want Malchas to be without an ear. Jesus touched his ear and healed him—But Jesus didn't heal me. Each night I felt the after-shock when my bed jumped from the floor and I woke with a start.

After the surgery, all I knew was the sound. Maybe it was the static of the universe that overshadowed my hearing ear. Maybe it was cosmic radiation outblasting my ear. Whatever it was—sound was bloated. It would lessen, the doctor told me, but it did not.

If only silence flanked me.

My father and uncle had warned us. Didn't we listen?

It was sound waves I rode. I struggled for balance. I felt the tilt of the earth. The tides of the ocean. I heard the whale's cry— \\\\ \\\ \\\\\\ \\\\\\\\ —One night watching television I saw the blast of a harpoon. The stream of blood. The whale's cry sounded like my own voice.

Boys in the neighborhood stayed away, but slowly they came back. I looked at them as though from underwater. I could see their mouths moving, but all I heard was the buzz of a motor boat headed into the distance.

The cousins stayed away for a while also. Maybe it was the large bandage on the side of my head.

A phantom sound haunted my ruptured eardrum. It disrupted the hearing ear. Each Sunday Miss Pinkney longed for a miracle to show everyone that Jesus still committed his acts of healing. But healing for me remained distant as the cries I sometimes heard in my missing ear.

In school, I couldn't understand what the teacher said. The teacher moved me to the front row, but that only made the noise worse. It only made louder what I couldn't understand.

I took medication. I had another surgery to graft skin on the burned spots on my head. I had lessons on how not to hear noise. How not to be terrified by explosions in the night. How not to let it bother me when people stared at my head—at the place where my ear had been.

I heard my father and uncle arguing. They had hard looks on their faces when they talked. It probably was about money. I heard my parents arguing. I thought what it must cost them. How much insurance. Who was responsible.

It all was defeat—even when my uncle came to the house with the older cousin, red-faced and shaking, to apologize. I knew he had been crying, which meant he had received a beating. There was no other way he would confess. I sat before my large cousin, not understanding his words, but knowing what he said—he snuck in a bottle-rocket, lit it, it tipped and flew into my head. I knew the cousin had not cried over what he had done, but that his father had forced the confession from him in front of his younger cousin. A bottle-rocket tipped and flew into my head—I knew the older cousin was repeating his confession. All the same—the cousin somehow conveyed defiance or the idea of defiance. He was only confessing because he had to. I could imagine the welts on my cousin's backside.

I couldn't hear, but I could see the feeling balled up in the spoken language. Words came packed with meaning I had never known. There were little explosions inside them. Words were fireworks.

Imagine—Miss Pinkney said—Jesus was with his disciples. The soldiers came to arrest him. Peter, always rash, drew his sword and, not knowing what else to do, severed an ear from a servant. Jesus was about to be arrested. He would go to the cross and suffer unspeakable agony—agony beyond description—and one of his disciples raised a sword and cut off an ear? What was a fisherman doing with a sword? Did he use it against the fish? Did he catch them by goring them?

I saw the students in the Sunday-school class snicker. I knew they'd heard another absurdity from Miss Pinkney. I was beginning to differentiate between expressions on those I saw—those things I was too busy to see before I was half-deaf. More than half.

Now Miss Pinkney was reading Leviticus 8:23—she showed me the passage. A priest carried the mark of blood on his ear. I was marked. I was a priest with blood on my ear. How exuberant she was—just like Peter getting in the way of what was happening. I wanted to be ignored, not noticed, but Miss Pinkney always was shining her light on me.

I didn't want to go to church, but it was preferable to a beating.

Next it was Amos 3:12—A shepherd took out of the mouth of the lion two legs and a piece of an ear—Where did she get this? Should Miss Pinkney be under scrutiny? Should the church authorities be alerted? I knew I was the sheep she meant. The explosion of a bottle-rocket was a lion that had my ear in its mouth. I felt it chewing. In my dreams—in my terrors of the night—I saw Miss Pinkney pull part of my ear from a lion's mouth.

One of the boys with an older brother said I would be exempt from military service. But the way my ear sounded, I already was in war.

The burned spots itched my head as they healed. I couldn't sit in class. I often was dizzy. I had headaches. It was all that noise. I couldn't understand. The bottle-rocket had confiscated my hearing. No, I could hear somewhat. It was the understanding of the hearing that had been replaced. The ear that didn't hear stood in the way of the hearing ear. The buzz in my deaf ear overrode any sound that would come through.

Miss Pinkney flew one way and another like a strange bird on a barren coast. Had there been complaints? Was it only me who objected as the object of her attention? What about her half-crazed exuberance? Her sword? Her breath of ice? The death. The shed blood. The whole of thbe story.

In my dizziness, I felt the flight over water. The slippery dreams. The engine in the ship. No, it couldn't be a ship. A ship did not have an engine. The whaling vessels were sailing ships. How confusing deafness was. Or partial deafness. All the elements that needed to shape my hearing were misshapen. What was this field-trip underwater?

I felt the little dogs, the rupturing of dogs breaking out in yapping. What were they doing? Were they the whale-station master's dogs?—poisoned like the neighborhood's dog that had howled all day before it died?

Maybe it was gale winds.

I had another surgery. I felt wrapped in blue. It was the ocean after all. And the sky that looked down upon it. I sank into the waves. I heard the water breathe. I learned to breathe as the water breathed. I turned my head and was dizzy again. Sometimes I fell. Sometimes I caught himself against a wall before I fell.

I took lessons to read lips, but I kept thinking he was watching the whale's mouth. I kept thinking I was hearing the ocean spill. I wanted to tell them there as another world—a subterranean world beneath the one everyone took for granted. How much depended on hearing. I took hand signals—sign-language lessons. I went to live with the water.

I liked to follow ships, though my whale parents told me they were dangerous. I should not get too near. They had harpoons that had taken many of our relatives.

Now I had a cane to balance me—the way the moon balanced the earth.

A whole story took all the different parts to tell what happened. The gospels needed to be read together to find which disciple was involved—and what the servant's name was—Miss Pinkney said. Jesus had just been betrayed and his unruly, rowdy unmanageable disciple cut off an ear. For what purpose? What did Peter intend?

My uncle and cousins came back to the house. The men played pinochle again. The women talked in the kitchen with its big, flowered curtains. The neighborhood seemed to move to the front and back porches once more. The older cousin, a bully in the past who had been subdued, was a bully again.

I would get used to hearing what was distorted and intercepted with noise. I drew the whale cries for the doctor.

\\\\\ \\ \ \ \\\\\.

Loomis was his name.
I kept drawing for the doctor.

Now it was?—What was that? Loomis asked.

Peter whacking his way through the net with his sword. That's why fish had no ears. I was talking in fragments—Baling water with a tin bucket from the ear-drum, the canal, the shore of the ear. I, a servant of the high priest, was a whale. It was Peter in a frantic moment not knowing what to do, drew his sword and whacked off an ear. Jesus picked it up and stuck it back on the whale's head.

After another surgery, I had an ear. Not an inside ear, but a prosthetic ear—a *pinna*. Some of the boys wanted to touch it.

Others stood back. I could tell by their faces how it must look. I knew the thoughts behind what they were saying. The boys seemed like fish to me.

How many whaling ships on the ocean had harpoons flying from them like Peter's sword?—How many swords whacking away belief, severing the roots of words. This little blast of language. This bottle-rocket.

Almost every night, I felt the explosion like a harpoon. In my dream, my ear fell off. They tried to sew it back on. It was a piñata on my head. There were continual bangings against it. They came like aftershocks.

The next fall, I was held back in school because I was behind. It was better, my father said. Then let my father watch his friends go on to the next grade while he remained behind.

The girl in the next seat in the new class got sick when she saw my head. The teacher moved me to the whale station in back of the class where I sat in isolation. Just one more thing to mark me as different.

My parents thought of sending me to a deaf school. No! I protested. It was a school where I could learn how many things I could hear without hearing. NO! I was an apostle of silence after my ear was crucified.

Loomis said that hair could be transplanted to the bald places on my head. Eventually I would look normal again—people behind me in class wouldn't cry. Eventually I would be myself.

Miss Pinkney approached me again in Sunday school.

I suffer your cause, O Lord.

\\\\ \\\\\\\ \\\\\\\\\\\\\ \ \\\\\\ \\ \\\\\.

Let me wash your feet with my fins.

\\\\ \ \\\\\\\\\ \\\\ \\.

The children were laughing. I lifted my fist and began hitting my ear. I hit and hit until the soldiers came to take me away. No, Miss Pinkney said—It was her they should arrest. I was the servant with my ear cut off. She was the one who should go to the cross. But the soldiers arrested me. They carried me from the room. The wrong one would go to the cross. The soldiers didn't get it right.

Miss Pinkney received a letter not to teach anymore. Someone sent their bottle-rocket at her. Someone harpooned her. Afterwards, she sat subdued in church. \\ \ \   \\\   \ \ \ \ \   \\ \ \ \
\ \ \ \ \ \ \\ \ \ \   \ \ \ \ \\   \ \   \ \ \   \ \   \ \ \ \   \\\\   \\\\ \ \ \
\     \\\ \ \ \ \ \ \   \ \ \                    \ \ \                        \ \
\                \.

Sometimes I thought she looked at me. Sometimes I thought
she heard the whale cries too. She had joined me in my amphibious
world. It was the cross we bore—separated from others in an ocean
of incongruities. Now she would know the hearing that was under
hearing. She would increase the possibilities of impossibilities.

As the universe started with a bang, it continued banging—I
was in the deaf school where I was sent far away. It was an act of
consecration, Miss Pinkney would have said.

Everything moved away from me faster than I could keep up
with. It was what I heard in the bottle-rocket of words. It was what
I heard in the little acts of violence in this mistaken world.

# THE ROUNDNESS OF EARTH

Sister Maria Jesus de Agreda, 1602–1655,

was born Maria Coronel y Arana in Agreda, Spain.

When her parents established a convent in their house,

her mother told Maria she would become a nun. She agreed.

She bilocated listening to the Alleluias during the Mass.

And their vibrations carried her—

*THE LADY IN BLUE*, JAVIER SIERRA


. . . on the face of the wilderness, there lay a small round thing.

—EZEKIEL 16:14 KJV

She didn't know when she began to levitate. She didn't do it on purpose. She was standing in the air above the ground as if there were no gravity to hold her down. She still had weight. She didn't fly off in the air—at that time anyway. Maybe it was a trial run— a seeing what could be done. An attempt at what would become flight. To see if she could manage it. She stood without her feet touching the ground. She wasn't frightened. She didn't think it strange. It was something that happened. There were others in the chapel. She heard their gasps. The nuns shunned her for a while. They didn't know what to do. Her levitation became something not spoken of, at least to her ears.

Now she was taking little hops over the convent wall. To the edge of the field. To a spot in the nearby woods. She always could see the convent. Or hear it. The prayers. The Alleluias of the nuns. Their clear voices rising to the air. Clapping against the leaves. Their voices were steps she could climb.

Now she was face down on the floor before the cross. Christ came at night when the quarter moon was a slice of pineapple. She felt the weight of the cross as if it was on her back. She began to see the feet of the beings of light that stayed in the room when she was before the cross. She assumed they were angels.

They were diligent—those angels that appeared. At first they were quiet. Then they spoke. They told her that people were in danger. They were in the way of someone coming.

Who would come? She asked.

They answered, the Spaniards, of course. The people would be hurt when the explorers arrived in their ships. The people would be killed. They had to be told of Christ before it happened. She had to go.

She didn't ask why the angels, or beings of light, didn't go by themselves. Why they wanted her as baggage. They had enough to carry—the chalices, the crosses, the rosaries.

Often in prayer, other places came to mind. She didn't know where they were. But she knew they were places that had not heard of Christ. Even the ground cried out. She must go to them. She thought her heavy garments and rosary and the cross she held would weigh her down. But she flew. The angels flew with her. Or she flew with them. Yet she remained where she was.

The nuns told her she never left the convent when she told her story of flight. It was different than levitation. But the nuns said she prayed with them. She stirred the soup. Stirring and stirring the beans. Otherwise they stuck to the bottom of the pot. Yet the wind was her passport, a word she didn't know, but it was there to be known.

Several angels traveled with her, knocking clouds out of the way. Changing altitudes. Changing lanes. The earth flickered as if it were a candle flame. She felt she was climbing narrow, drafty steps.

Then the waves below them were pointed and choppy as the shell of a pineapple.

I tell you, the music traveled with us. I heard it in the air. If I felt myself waver, I lifted my eyes and listened to the sound.

There were thick forests on the other side of the sea. Then wide places of hardly any trees. There were rivers of different sizes in different places. Then the land climbed up into mountains. Then the land flattened into desert. This is where they landed with a clunk.[1]

The angels said there were people there something like the Romani they called gypsies who wandered in Spain. They were dark. They were painted. They wore feathers and animal skins. They were horrific in their practices. They were called, the Jumano.

1. The desert southwest of America

She talked to the people in their own language. It was a language she didn't know. She told them of the Savior. At night, the stars crawled with lice. He is a Savior with a long tongue. He licks our wounds and the discomforts of our bites.

Sometimes she spoke to them in her own language, and they seemed to understand.

She remained in the convent while she was gone. No one could be in two places at once. But she was. Others had been transported. Or was it teleported? Enoch—Genesis 5:24, Elijah—II Kings 2:11, Philip—Acts 8:39—were travelers in the Bible. But were they in two places at once? She traveled in a blue light. She didn't know how long it took. On the trips, she saw the people before her. It was as if they waited for her. Did they know she was coming? No. But they were there waiting. Or had she simply projected an image of herself descending from the air trailing spots of light? It seemed sometimes she spoke to them without moving her mouth.

Now she was face down on the floor of the convent in agonies of sorrow for the strange people.

In-two-places-at-once. The name they gave her in the convent when she told them she'd been to a desert. She was aware of the washing of beans in a basin. She felt the ladle turning and turning in her hand, yet she saw the blue of the sky and waves as she flew to the other land.

Often when she traveled with the angels, they arrived at dusk. She saw the people gathered before her. She saw their dusty feet. Their faces ignorant of heaven.

I belong to you, Lord, she prayed. You are worthy of praise. You are magnificent. You carry me over the deep. I fly, not knowing where I am going. Your billows and waves pass under me. You died for my salvation. You were bitten by evil. Stung on the cross.

Sister Maria Jesus de Agreda then spoke to the people. I see the coming darkness for you. Flames will lick your body. They will not stop. Hell is beyond words in its horror. It is never over. The tribe of the Jumano looked at her. They cried. They howled. But there is salvation, she called to them. The angels spoke to some of the more hysterical ones. Pay attention, here. We're on this earth to meet Jesus—To be transformed into his likeness. To be both here and there with him. To know his suffering and to suffer with him. To escape from Hell. The eternity in Christ will more than make up for this tawdry existence. The roundness of this earth is in God.

She dreamed of the Jumano. She prayed for their transformation. She dreamed Jesus kissed their heads. In heaven, she knew she would meet some of them. They would be out with the angels, looking over their new land.

On her return to the convent, though she also never left it, she saw a turtle lumbering across the ground. She saw the marks of mud swirls on its shell. It looked like the earth below her when she traveled in the air. She wanted to say, he who made the pineapple also made the turtle.

Sometimes she flew far above the earth in its atmosphere. She made notes of her travels. He sits on the circle of the earth—Isaiah 40:22. The roundness had something to do with its rolling or moving. Or the ability to move. But round meant incomplete. Or lacking in fullness or completeness, as in rounding off a number.

No, they would make round trips, the angels said. They would be complete. Words were composed of those disagreeing parts. In the convent, the nuns made rounds of prayers. The beads they turned in their fingers were round. When they sang, their voices rolled like the earth. It was then she felt the little passageways open—the disagreeing parts of being here and there. It was then she flew to another place while remaining in the convent. She heard the music as she flew. It was the music that was the wings of her flight.

She knew whoever came to the land she visited would claim it for their own. She knew others would follow the Spaniards across the ocean—all of them trampling down whatever had been.

In the convent, she lived in a small, dull cell where she withdrew to pray for the suffering world. Spain was locked in its Inquisition. Sometimes in her prayers, she heard the tortured, the burned-at-the-stake. The church said the Inquisition was to get rid of the Moors. The Muslims. The heretics. The blasphemers. Sometimes she picked up the fear of being pointed to as a heretic because of her concern for the Jumano. It was palpable as a cloud of flies.

How often the angels told her they traveled the earth looking for those who would listen to them. What odd beings they were. Both solid and abstract. A chalice and a voyage. Their trips were guided by concern for the lost. They thought of others. Not themselves.

God is a wind that circles. That was her knowledge from travel. The humming ocean. The round earth with its patterns she heard in the music that turned into flight.

# THE SIMILITUDE OF OXEN

. . . he made a melted sea . . . And under it was the similitude of oxen.

II CHRONICLES 4:2–3


And he made a melted sea . . . And it stood upon twelve oxen, three looking toward the north, and three looking toward the west, and three looking toward the south, and three looking toward the east, and the sea was set upon them, and their rear sections were pointed inward.

I KINGS 7:23–25

The first owner of the land signed the land deed with an x because she couldn't write, not even to sign her name. There was nothing in the new language that could represent it. Not even a similitude. She was an Indian, probably Osage. She didn't sign by choice, but was forced or coerced to sell. There was not a place to leave her story. But the land carried it—the way the Salt Plains near Jet, Oklahoma carries the memory of the sea that once rolled on the prairie.

The versions of the salt field—

1. In the beginning there was a glacier. When the glacier melted, there was an ocean. When the ocean evaporated, there was a salt field.

2. Before the glacier, there was nothing. The Indians disagreed. There was another world before the nothing. It was in the cave drawings and petroglyphs. It was the images the dreamer saw in dreams. A visual state. A likeness of that other world.

3. There was a glacier. Then an ocean on the basin of the prairie floor. A warrior with a bow and arrow shot the edge of the glacier. It began to recede. There was a shore, and then a salt field when the water finally dried up. The tribes came there for salt. Or the memory of the ocean that used to be there.

4. In the beginning, there was a glacier on the great plains. Then a pool of water called an inland ocean. The Maker swept the water into bowls. He moved buffalo herds across the prairie and set the bowls upon their backs. The buffalo carried them. That's why there's a hump on their backs. That's why their

heads are low on their necks as if slipped from their high shoulders, as if their heads were sinking, as if the weight of all those memories was too much. Millions of them eventually killed by soldiers on passing trains.

After the glacier melted, the buffalo drank the water.
To this day, the buffalo are an evaporated ocean.

The buffalo speak—
We felt the little bones of rain. But what were these pellets? These ——— ? rolled into balls splayed over us. We were hit with knots from the tops of prairie grass. Burrs got into our skin and ripped out wires to our heart. But these were not puff balls.
The soldiers Pow. Pow. Pow.

I found the line dividing Kansas from Nebraska marked by stones . . . I [plotted] off two streets . . . east-west, north-south . . . laid foundation for 4 log houses . . . Indians burned the houses down . . . E.C. Manning, April 1860.

In 1864, Col. Chivington massacred a confederation of several hundred Indians at Sand Creek. There was a flurry of messages.
The Indians retaliated, butchering settlers, stampeding cattle, burning crops. They were dog soldiers, the Cheyenne resistance to encroachment. Roman Nose refused to sign treaties, seceding hunting grounds for a reservation in Indian territory. In 1867, Roman Nose tried to join Red Cloud, this time pursued by Gen. Eugene Carr.

It had looked like a treaty, but it wasn't. It looked like history, but it wasn't what it seemed in books, in school, but had worm-holes, alternate histories, different versions.
It looked like love, but it was broken too.

Settlers continually harassed by Indians. Dot. Dash. Dot. Dot. Dash. There were drive-bys, drive-offs. Gen. S.R. Curtis' telegraph to Chivington—Pursue everywhere and punish the Cheyenne and Arapahoe. Pay no attention to district lines.

The last Indian war in Kansas, September 27, 1878. 284 braves, women and children made a last stand at Ladder Creek in the northwest corner of Kansas.

Chivington's 1883 speech—Was Sand Creek a massacre? If it was, we had massacres almost without number during the late rebellion. That there may have been some excesses committed on the field, no one will deny. Was there ever a battle fought in which no excesses were committed?

Chivington's later footnote—The misrepresentation of this whole affair from the beginning was a combination consisting of one man who was disappointed of promotion and some others who were aspirants for office and wanted several connected with the campaign out of their way.

I'm sending this fax—This similitude of a telegraph. This report from my side of the battle field. This similitude of a story.

Sometimes on winter nights, I get out my scrapbook and look at the past.

In 1874, in Meade County, Kansas, northwest of the Salt Plains, Cheyenne killed six government surveyors who were marking off buffalo-hunting land. The Cheyenne carried a similitude of their murdered relatives at Sand Creek, which was revenge. Oliver Short wrote to his wife the night before he was killed, and sent the letter with passing buffalo hunters to mail the next morning. That day, the Cheyenne spotted Oliver Short, age 41, his son, Daniel, age 14, James Shaw, age 51, Shaw's son, Allen, about 18, John Keuchler, 18, and Harry Jones, early 20s. Another friend or two of Allen's from Kansas University had stayed in the main camp.

When another team of surveyors discovered them, the skulls of three men were crushed, two were scalped. Oliver Short's compass was smashed into his forehead.

On January 26, 1875, Mrs. O.F. Short, widow of Short, wrote Captain Miles a letter from Lawrence, Kansas. *My spirit is burdened with gratitude for the intelligence communicated by Supt. Hoag of the surrender of the Indians who murdered my husband. By faith I almost hear the details. Mrs. Shaw spent the night with me, and in her grief, I could almost forget my own. Allen. Allen, is all she could say.*

*My dear sir, could you indulge us in a few questions?*

  i) *Were the Indians waiting for the surveyors?*

  ii) *Was one man killed at first attack? Was it the compass man?*

  iii) *Were all the boys killed in the wagon?*

  iv) *Who was the last one alive? Was it Mr. Shaw, the teamster? We heard of his haphazard boot prints around the wagon.*

  v) *Were any Indians killed or wounded?*

In the end, the sea was on hooves.

    Zrrrrr.

The blackrobes came with a small man on a cross they wore on their belts.

    The buffalo believed the man on the cross was not big enough to matter. They did not raise their heads from the grass. They did not see the waves of soldiers in the grass. They were caught unaware.

    More soldiers Pow. Pow. Pow.

    Then settlers came with their covered wagons, their miner's picks, their tooth extractors, their tinfoil sky. The little soldiers dancing the rumba. Sometimes Indians shoving back.

The prairie fills the map. Is there anything but grasslands? Prairie grass after prairie grass? The similitude of borders.

In 1877, Mrs. Short wrote again asking for money—I am sorry to feel again the necessity of intruding upon your time but I feel that something must be done to help me through the summer with my little ones . . .

It is noted that she received help, though none of the starving survivors of the Sand Creek and Washita massacres and other raids on Indian camps did, though they partitioned the government.

In 1867, the buffalo began hearing voices. It was not other buffalo, though it sounded like grunting. The wind was swift. The buffalo were not at all interested in the voices. They had their own agenda. Carrying the burden of the melted ocean on their backs.

The buffalo were offered sanctuary by the blackrobes in exchange for their knowledge—How they could hold their calves in a late blizzard. How they followed their unmarked trails. How nothing stood in the way of their resolution. But the buffalo thought they said backrobe and thought their own coat was sufficient. They ignored the man on the cross. When his side was pierced, smoke came out like a smoke bomb. Azure was the vivid of all the vivids.

There are reasons they were killed—Herds of buffalo crossing the railroad tracks. The Indians depended upon their lives.

It is the art of water. To leave residue in its wake.

Over the years, I made a treaty with my memory—You take the past. I take the present. I signed it with an x.

I live in a house in a succession of occupants on borrowed / stolen land. I can't row against the current of this new world. I don't have a river.

The versions of love—A Sunday afternoon, upriver, two people together, rowing. Only the similitude of a relationship. It would not last, but the love would. Or what seemed like love. Yet I attacked it as if it was a wagon train. I rode against occupation.

The memory of it a snapshot in the album of the mind. The stars fought against us. Hailstones came from the sky. We covered our heads with a thin jacket. We rowed back to the shore. It had been after a weekend when others left. But our time together was over too. We continued to write, to call. But it was a thin trail of smoke above the campfire that finally went out.

Love was the only oar we had. Everything else was broken.

It was a misrepresentation. My late rebellion in the relationship. Or maybe the question, rebellion in whose point-of-view? It was the massacre of my heart that would not love again, but continue its hollow beating.

He made a molten sea and under it was the buffalo. By he, I mean the glacier. I was not there to see it, but by its evidence, I know it was there.

The salt field is the similitude of a glacier—well, a flat glacier. The snowy field of a glacier—looking all white in the distance, but streaked and stained up close.

I often wonder what I have built on misconception and error.

After the blackrobes—the missionaries built their own churches with their versions of faith. They each thought they were the ones God liked. Maybe he changed his mind or he changed or couldn't decide between them all because they all had a lot of versions. They each had their own way to say what they said. There were all kinds. They did not always like each other. They didn't always talk. They seemed to ignore one another, yet they all brought God.

All the time, Hallelujah. Hallelujah. They sang like that.

The versions of history keep interrupting—

I follow their trail into the wilderness, which my thinking is. I have a handle on myself. I know how the water is.

This letter I leave. This land deed.

A blackish wind still dancing the rumba after the little soldiers moved on.

The 1877 Council of the Buffalo:

What can be said of the humped-backs of the prairie? The brown furry ones with small rears and scraggly tails like a splintered oar? Various tribes gathered. They could ride into battle. They could retreat and do nothing. The prophets, those holders of the sea, those pumped-up ones, in front, at least, gave council: It would be the same no matter what the Indians did.

Utilitarian buffalo. Industrial sized. After railroads, land grants, section lines, fences, settlements, towns. The buffalo were sent to buffalo boarding schools showing them their new world called, extinction.

After several years, the buffalo left the boarding school— warped and hybrid. I almost said hybird because they now fly high above the salt field. The white clouds rolled. They are just under the azure ghost of an old sea sloshing in a bowl. They are making buffalo wallets to sell for souvenirs.

The whole history of the prairie moves across the land—turbulent as the azure wars in our past—right here in the middle of our land. Almost unknown—those worm-hole events in the historical mode. They are there waving in the tall grasses. The land carries memories of what passed there. I pick them up in images and fragments, the way the body of Lt. Lyman Kidder was identified by his father from a scrap of the shirt his mother had made after the Kidder massacres by Sioux and Cheyenne in 1867 in the northwest corner of Kansas.

The land hears voices. The land stores them. The land carries them. The land is a library. A museum. History is deposited there. The land is a voice speaking the plains. The great plains.

The buffalo still hold the sea. When it rains, I know they are migrating to another pasture. They never hold still. In dreams I see buffalo transporting water. They are the irrigation wheels I see from the plane.

I hold the buffalo in a glass globe. I turn it upsidedown and they float back to earth. I show the globe—but all anyone sees is the snow. Don't you hear the past? Don't you see what happened? The point of this? The purpose? The underlayers of what is over? The present always is a similitude of the past.

Sometimes on winter nights, I get out my scrapbook and look at his letters. These representations of our relationship. Ticket stubs, memorabilia. Old photos, though there are not many. Snapshots representing the snap of a relationship—the final shot. Did we look happy, even then?

What happened to the relationship? I spent a great deal of time in the past. He was concerned over what he called my preoccupation. He loved more than me. What else could I do? I could not recover from history. I was a facsimile of myself.

I loved the rattle of his boat on the trailer behind his car on our way to the lake. Some nights I send smoke signals hoping they will reach.

I believe the storms are spirits riding on the backs of buffalo. I hear their voices calling me—I don't know where they are coming from—Across what district line.

In storms, I am the thunderee, the one who receives the noise, the fright. The sky is the thunderer. I hear those voices that ride the storms: We signed away our land with an *x*. They gave us—rifle, blanket, kettle, tobacco, compensation for property abandoned, cost of emigration.

The cluck of thunder. That chickenyard sky.

I was not made for this world.

My flag unfurled.

I made a treaty with my memory. I am now one person rowing. My head is a glacier. When it melts the world will flood. After which I will become a pillar of salt. I live in a house with indentions along side the door. I know the people who lived in the house before me had a dog who wanted in most of its life. That's the way it is.

At night, I hear the buffalo scratching. At night I feel my fingers on the wall.

Everyone trying to reach someone they have lost. Or left.

I continued to think of that old world I feel floating at my ankles whenever I walk through the similitude of prairie grass.

We carry their histories within us. Someone else will carry ours.

# THE LAST INDIAN WAR
# IN KANSAS

In 1876, at the end of the Plains Indian wars, U.S. Calvary troops from Fort Leavenworth rounded up Northern Cheyenne in Kansas and moved them to a reservation in Indian Territory (which later became Oklahoma). Two years later, 89 braves, 112 women and 134 children escaped from the reservation and traveled to northwest Kansas, killing 40 settlers and terrorizing counties along the way. Troops from Fort Leavenworth finally arrived, killing most of the Indians, and returning the rest to the reservation in Indian Territory. Historical markers in northwest Kansas give their different versions of the war.

Roffo sold venison pizza at his road house. The deer meat was from Dull Knife's where a hunter could take his deer and receive it back packaged and frozen. Roffo used wild onions and a few pine nuts on the government-surplus commodity cheese.

Edgar and Herman drove the reservation roads delivering Roffo's pizzas.

On the road, they heard the last Indian war in Kansas. Northern Cheyenne fleeing to their old hunting ground for their lives. Over 100 years ago. They had been moving targets.

If they fought. If they surrendered. What did it matter? The end was the same for all—A quick death outnumbered on the battlefield, or a slow starvation on the reservation.

At times, Edgar thought the dull roar they heard could be the interstate in the distance, which followed an old military road, but Herman decided it was too far. He thought instead of the low snorting of a buffalo herd in the dark—a ghost herd—It was a low, almost soundless noise they heard when they stopped the car on the reservation road as they did sometimes to look at the sky above them round as a pizza pan—where stars sparked like wild onions.

The last Indian raid. The last Indian war. The name, place and numbers varied on various road-side markers and plaques. It took place along Sappa Creek. Ladder Creek. Cherry Creek. It took place in the counties of Rawlins, Cheyenne, Decatur, Osborne. It happened near the towns of Oberlin and Kanona, or St. Francis on the South Fork of the Republican River. Was everyone trying to shuffle it off on someone else? Or did they want to be the ones that ridded Kansas of Indians? The victims were Kansas settlers murdered on their farms—In Decatur County, 19 were killed on

Sappa Creek. Or was it Osborne County? There were 335 Northern Cheyenne on the rampage—Or 284. The last Indian war was not in one place, but spread over counties, across creeks, even state lines to Nebraska and Montana.

What of it? What of it?—They thought on the road. The hopeless repetition of nights that would pass in poverty and hopelessness—In knowing no rescue was on the way.

Now Edgar and Herman arrived at Thoroughgood's hut—who didn't have his monies together—always seemed surprised that Edgar and Herman wanted paid—seemed to think they would deliver venison pizza and drive off. They had to wait while Thoroughgood drove to Wilford's. Then he had to drive to Uncle Murtha's and meanwhile Edgar and Herman found a dollar under the seat cushion in the kitchen where Thoroughgood had an old car-seat pushed to the table for a chair. The pizzas still to be delivered getting cold—they warmed them in the oven while Thoroughgood was gone—came back short—couldn't find the money his wife was saving for beads. Said Happy might have money. Edgar and Herman left the pizza with him—their car broke down just short of Happy's. They had to walk back to Roffo's, leaving undelivered pizzas in the car.

In the distance, they heard the coyotes howl. There was another call above the sound of the highway they were too far away to hear—a wolf or a wild dog, or the buffalo or some ancestor calling them on. They also had parents and relatives who would not return from wherever they had gone. Sometimes late at night, they would hear a car on the road making a run for it.

Let the spirits flying over the reservation at night deliver the rest of the pizzas.

In the road house, Roffo was on the phone with everyone still expecting a pizza delivery. At the table, Edgar held a butter knife in one hand by its handle. With his other hand, Edgar pulled the knife back with the blade end, letting go as if flinging something through the air. The way a food fight would start if there was enough food to fight.

Edgar was flinging the lost voice of the land he and Herman brought in with them from the road. They could go with it—If they were thin as a pine nut—If they were as thin as truth.

Indians had been on the plains of America, though it didn't have that name at the time. The Great Plains of America. That was their place. They were defined by the western edge of Kansas where their ancestors had ridden, taking lives in their anger, and their fury at being replaced. They had swept across homesteads and helpless settlers there. It was on the road markers—All giving their side of the versions of the truth. They had raped, murdered, scalped, burned.

The anger was still there in Edgar, Herman, and everyone they knew. They talked of what they could have been if they hadn't been stopped. But what could they have done?

Roffo's oven always was overheating or underheating. It was as variable as the last Indian war. But Edgar and Herman knew the last Indian war in Kansas was the battle with alcohol, which Roffo also served.

When Wilford drove out to Happy's and got their car working again, Edgar and Herman left it parked at Roffo's with its nose facing the street, making it look like they had someplace in a hurry to go. And they did. They also were volunteer auxiliary firemen. There always was a brushfire on the reservation. A smoking gun. A heater that exploded. A car engine. Trash barrels. Sheds burned. The stars burned. Sometimes Wilford went on a revolt and they hosed him down.

Sometimes a jet passed high above them with the roar of a barrel fire.

It was an enormous, great dark sky after the sun went out.

When they delivered pizzas, Edgar and Herman rode the high plains where they wanted to be. They took part in the revenge. When they returned from their deliveries, they relived their raids at Roffo's. Soldiers had been called from Fort Leavenworth for the last Indian war. They could hear the echoes of their horses coming.

Edgar didn't like the round, little beads of wild onions on his pizza. He placed them one by one on the dull blade of his knife, pulling it back, letting go, as if catapulting them all to safety.

# THE STORM THAT
# LOVED A BIKE

My grandmother, Molly McGivern, had a small walnut bed and side-table with one drawer in a back-room off the kitchen. I slept there as a child. It seems now I remember her baking biscuits in the mornings; the smell waking me. I had a wash-and-wear mother who'd married a Pottawatomie man, or part-Pottawatomie, he said. Pottawatomie and some French. I was the street sweeper that came along behind her. Paul Samuel was the Christian name my father had received in boarding school. My cousins lived with their parents, their mother being my mother's sister. Their mother was the sister who stayed married, whose husband did not leave her because they were of European descent and lived decently in the center of town. Only the Indians left their wives and families on the edge of Arkansas City—my mother wanting him to leave most of the time, but when he finally left, it devastated her.

On the walnut side-table was a doily and a lamp. The bulb was so dim it cast a yellow light in the room pale as the paper in the bottom of the drawer. My grandmother let me keep in the drawer: marbles, a twig, whatever I found. Some paper and a pencil. The Bible was on the side table also. Sometimes I read Ezekiel for his visions of cherubim. My grandmother was a Christian who let me know it was her Christian duty to keep me. I was the dark side of the light. The shadow. The black sheep that Jesus sought. At school I was ignored. Except for one girl from our church, it being her duty also. If there was a party I was not invited, but I heard the girls discussing it before and after.

On the walnut bed was a green quilt with a pattern of yellow and brown flowers. It was a small floral pattern I used to look at it. I kept my clothes in a lump on the floor. At one time, the room must have been a storage room or pantry. My mother breezing into the house now and then between boyfriends until after loud arguments and slaps, my grandmother wouldn't let her return. I was the low-water scum they talked about behind my back. I would fidget at my desk. My mind jumped from one thing to another. I couldn't light anywhere.

My grandmother had a house full of what would now be antiques. Walnut and oak and one of the chests I remember my aunt saying was cherry. When my grandmother died, the dealers came for everything. My aunt stayed angry at my mother because of the way the furniture was dispersed. Somehow the dealers knew my mother was the one to approach about the sale of the pieces. I don't remember how my mother could sell them with my aunt standing over her, but it happened. My aunt is dead now and sometimes when I leave flowers at the graves, I think I hear her say, your mother sold the furniture for nothing.

That was the final break between them. The upstanding family and the one in fragments with a child who was dark as her father in a light family, some with hair that was almost white when they were children, though it darkened to blonde.

Who knew how many places my grandmother's things were? It always haunted my mother's sister. Maybe it was a way to get back at her sister for marrying a man who stayed with her.

I guess it was the usual story: a young woman running away from home to marry a man also on the run from a normal life. It was something outside of his realm. He never knew what it was, and if he did, he would have run faster than my mother. It broke my grandparent's heart; my grandfather a doctor and all. He demanded dinner sometimes when he returned home late in the evening. I remember the smell of frying chicken after dark, their voices outside my back-room. He made house calls and hospital visits and my grandmother fed him afterwards, even if it meant cooking another full meal after she had fed us—her and me, and sometimes a neighbor in need or someone from church. They came through our house all the time. Finally, my grandmother got back at him by dying.

My mother had a firm foundation, though she departed from it. My father had nothing. I knew little about him. He paced the kitchen of our house, usually ended up throwing something at my mother. He was caged in a world where he didn't belong. How do you face what you don't want to do? I knew that too. But I had my grandparent's steady life that pulled me back from running. When my grandmother died, she left some money earmarked, Polly Samuel's education. That was all it could go for. If I didn't go to college, the money would be added to the college funds of my cousins. That was all I needed to know.

I remembered my father's lack of focus. If he met friends, he wouldn't be back until he remembered us. If someone called, he was gone, no matter what had been planned. He always was sidetracked. He did not have steady work. There was tension between him and my grandparents that sawed them all in half.

I have lived in fear of his driftfulness. I too ran from Kansas to Minnesota to Texas and back, starting out sometimes not knowing where. I had no one to lean on, no one to turn to. What do you do when you're in it by yourself? I decided to learn responsibility. I would do what my parents could not. I would stop running. I would be responsible for myself. It had its drawbacks. I did the clean-up after grandma's death, all those things no one else would do. I waxed the floors after the rugs were taken up. I carried her jars from the cellar, and her old magazines from the attic. My grandmother had left me money. I owed it to her. I went to college in Wichita the fall after I finished high school. I hated it, and decided to run from it too, but there was a conference, *The Native American Experience*, and it kept me there. I heard a man talk about the early Fort Michili-mackinac and the Mackinac-Prairie du Chien trails for fur trade in the northern territory. I thought maybe my father had been Menominee or Menominee-Winnebago instead of Pottawatomie because the man reminded me of him. I heard another panel on the southern removal trails. I heard the distances that my father's people had covered. The names Crow Wing and Oshkosh washed over me, the names of the past I belonged to, in part, anyway.

The walnuts ran away from the tree, I made up stories. They fell on the ground where they landed, something like my mother who would write from one place or another when she had enough money she'd send for me.

Things didn't turn out like she expected, she said to me once. What did she expect?—Leaving her parent's house with a wild man.

I never knew my father's people. He took me to see them once or twice. There was a house somewhere on open land. No one said anything. My mother had been lured by the mystique of buckskin and images of brown warriors, braves and chiefs, the whole Winnebago line. She must have known right away it wouldn't work, but kept at it until I was born.

My Grandmother McGivern and I would pick up walnuts on a corner lot. I saw the walnuts, their ridged shells. How did they make a bed and side-table from that? I knew the furniture was made from the wood of the tree, but I wanted to believe it was from the shells. I thought of them sending their workers into the field, gathering walnuts, returning to the furniture factory. In the thunder, I thought I heard them pounding walnuts, pounding and pounding out the ridges for long nights after. I thought of the magic that changed the walnuts into furniture, that was important enough for my aunt to be angry with my mother the rest of her life. I thought of the knobbed head and foot rails of the bed, the knobbed legs of the side-table. The walnuts had run away from the tree. They were taken from the ground where they landed.

My aunt came to my mother's funeral. She stood in the back and didn't say anything. The minister told us that Marsha McGivern Samuel was in the hereafter covered by Jesus' blood. And he asked if anyone wanted to say something, and no one did, and I thought it was my place, being her daughter. I said she was my mother and I remembered the flowered dress she wore that touched my face when she leaned down to tell me that she would be back tomorrow or the tomorrow after that.

If I could have any job, I would be a fire-eater in a traveling sideshow. I would be from Colstrip, Montana, or Ten Sleep,

Wyoming. But I was not any of that. I was from Arkansas City in southern Kansas, just off I-35. I was in college, and had papers to write, and books to read I didn't want to read. In desperation, I hitchhiked to another town, hitchhiked back, crying into my bed because I had to stay in school. I felt my father's need to flee. I felt my grandmother's gumption. I learned to make lesson plans and charts of whatever the instructor of the course asked for. I would rather have heard my parents scream at one another.

After graduation, the only offer I received was from a college on the edge of a great lake teaching six courses of freshman composition every semester and summer. I moved from Kansas to Duluth in a row of clapboard houses on a hill, ugly and grim as the climate itself. Behind in the alley, were ice-fishing houses with peeling paint. The clapboard weather, gray, cold, windy, was as hard to take as the Kansas heat. I heard the call of gulls for some-one to take them away.

We had learned about the Indians hunting buffalo in grade school. My father was Pottawatomie. I didn't know if the Pot-tawatomie hunted buffalo, though I imagined they did. My mother was of German and Irish descent, another mix of heritages with boll weevils in it. But I was on the margins of it all. I was born in the days there was no multicultural recognition. No talk of mixed-heritages or displacement on the borderlands. I did not speak the Indian language. I did not have the land. I did not know the old relationship to the Maker, though I knew there was relationship. I was the usual mix: German, Irish, French and Pottawatomie. I was even born in a town that had the name of another state. Arkansas City, Kansas. Not Ark-an-saw, like the nearby state, but Ar-kansas.

My father hadn't come to the McGivern house unless he was drunk or nearly so. My cousins laughed at him. I remember once we rode in my grandfather's Pontiac looking for my father, my grandfather thinking he could form him into a family man, the way walnuts were transformed into furniture.

I was outside the main culture. I was outside the minority culture. I wasn't an Indian, though I had Indian blood. I wasn't white. Where was my place? If *place* defined one. Where were the ruins of the past that over-shadowed my present? I knew the blurring of boundaries. I knew the borders. Where was the land I was from? Who were my people? Plurality was my nationality. I was more than two in one.

If only it was easy and not a matter of visions. Traveling between Minnesota and my family in Kansas, the few times I visited the cousins, up and down I-35 dangling like a string. A zip-way to the northern shores. The next world coming. Already here. The sky ripped up. I stopped in Kansas for the only toll gate. $6.75. How can they do that? The renovation of a country. The fractured place swept out, dusted, spray-painted. Pushed together. Spliced. Grafted—until what was it?—The first wave of the new stress? Taking a potshot at intercultural inexactness. Everything rattling that was not nailed down. How could any of them understand others? What made sense about cultures?

In my composition classes in Duluth, I had boys who hated English. Who hated writing. Who would not, could not write a sentence without chopping it up. I knew how they felt. They were not minority or mixed-blood, but they were outside the group of learners who could pass through classes and graduate. There was a program on television, Orange County Choppers, where a family, the Teutul's, made custom-built motorcycles. I heard the boys talking about it, and watched the program myself. I told them they could write essays on that program. A motorcycle is an act of composition, I told the students.

The wheels of a motorcycle are Biblical. I read about the cherubim in the first chapter of Ezekiel—He saw a whirlwind come from the north. A fire enfolded the whirlwind, and the fire was a great headlight. Out of the fire and the wind came other riders. They had wings, and under their wings were handlebars. They rode motorcycles and their wheels were full of eyes. Wherever the spirit went, they went. They were like burning coals of fire, shining with headlights. They rode as if flashes of lightning.

The composition students listened to Ezekiel. They watched Orange County Choppers on television. They listened to my visions of cherubim that were motorcycles. The students saw the composition of their papers as design and fabrication. They did research, planned an outline, made a cardboard cutout, and so to speak, used duct tape. They were under pressure to get it done. They particularly thought writing was like welding. They jerked their head forward, and their face masks fell over their face. To be honest with you, their sparks flew in a vision of nouns and verbs. They welded thesis statement, development and conclusion.

I didn't know what happened to my father, though I could understand his dislocation, his disparate spirit, his isolation and desperation. I went to a Pottawatomie cemetery in the country, but never found his name. Maybe his family buried him by his Pottawatomie name, the one I didn't know. I've stopped in other cemeteries on trips, but he was never there.

Sometimes I drive on my own to see the pines, the walnuts, the birch.

The Christians made the Indians strangers to their own land. They made them strangers to their language. They made them strangers to their ceremonies. They made them strangers to others. They made them strangers to themselves. Bi-marginal Christianity. Itself a vectoring of marginalities. How does anyone understand?

Where are the altitudes? Latitudes? The geographies we pass through? Where are our dreams and visions? Our minds are story-makers, story-tellers. There's a place in our mind like a closet where dreams and visions are kept. A dream sees into the spirit world.

When I had visions of motorcycles, I prayed before the class, give us a place among the *being*-ones.

Why do we need dreams, even the bad ones? They help us remember there is more than we see. They help us see into the other world. We need our dreams to remind us. The bad dreams help us protect ourselves, to know the possibilities of harm exists. To not take our safety for granted. To haunt us so we look for an-swers. They make us face our fears. They make us know ourselves. Dreaming is like going to the movies, but we are the film-makers.

I eat fire in my dreams.

I was a fire eater in another way than I wanted. I faced five days a week in composition classes. I graded papers nights and weekends. My life was in the furnace of composition. My running now was to academic conferences. I could say a mixed-blood heritage is dislocation, but I couldn't find the form in which to display that dislocation until I wrote a paper, The *Bi-Marginality of Design in the Construct of Motorcycle Fabrication*. It was published in an academic journal.

I wrote it between composition classes in the cold dampness of my small, drafty office I shared with colleagues off Lake Superior. This is a look into the structure of another culture. Another world. I had a woven knit skirt, and when I turned it over, the pattern looked completely different. The underside was its counterplane. I wrote the underside of Indian language in English. It was all I could do.

I think of it when I eat fire.

You can't write about a boring life in a boring way, but can you shape dislocation with dislocation? I would say, yes.

And what of this love, this engine blast, this passion that carries a rider? Where did it come from? Discouraged in school since the beginning, the boys barely making it through, but going nonetheless because of the hope of what was on the other end.

Once, a storm saw a motorcycle, and fell in love. Its thunder was a voice trying to speak the language of the bike.

I heard motorcycles at night, though I knew they were snow removal trucks. The neighbor down the street had a motorcycle he rode even in the frigid weather. Sometimes I heard him going by on the road. He had a cycle-shop past the truck-stop. Thereafter, the road unfolded across Lake Superior. Even heaven had motorcycles. I heard them in the storms. That's why I knew I could trust God. His cherubim rode bikes. Maybe his cherubim were bikes.

A motorcycle was fury. It was passage. On summer nights, I saw the shiny waves along the shore ripple like oilcloth. I had a vision of this cross-cultural world.

I got out of bed and looked at the sky during a storm. I loved the passionate wind. The bright flash of light on the lake. The different voices of the thunder. Each night I heard the choppers that rode the whirlwind. I heard the hum of traffic, turning down for an exit at the truck stop, to fill with gas or sleep for the night.

A motorcycle was a gift from the spirit world. A motorcycle was a landscape passing. A motorcycle was a lighthouse. It was a shore for those great lakes on the map hanging like three hornets' nests from a branch. The wheels of a motorcycle were twirlers before a marching band.

A motorcycle was radiance.

A motorcycle waged war.

A motorcycle was a warrior.

A motorcycle was a desperado.

A motorcycle was a choice.

In church, the men passed the collection plate like a hubcap.

A motorcycle was a choir.

When the motorcycles understood what they were, they wept.

I understood that a motorcycle was a visit from the sacred world—if I honored it, if I spoke to it as a blueprint, a map of design, an abbreviation of something holy.

A motorcycle would help the students find the way to where they would go. In writing, they were as they knew they could be.

In the beginning (1885 I told them), a German, Gottlieb Daimler, invented an internal combustion engine and placed it on a frame with two wheels. That self-propelled vehicle was the first motorcycle.

I had a vision of how much could be imagined.

As they rode, the long shiny waves of the lake rippled like oilcloth.

I have longed for a husband from time to time. But it never worked. No one wanted to share my meal. When I was in school, the boys used to think they could take advantage of me even though my grandfather was Dr. McGivern and had removed the tonsils of most of them.

The Bible was dislocation. It was for those of mixed-heritage. It was a contradiction of bi-marginality. It was discontinuity.

Disruption. The differing voices telling the different stories. No one telling the same story.

My grandmother, Molly McGivern, knew the use of disruptives. If she saw me concentrating, she interrupted me, trying to subvert my interest in finding out. I learned in spurts, doing several things at once, covering up the concentration I wanted. It affected my academic writing, my pedagogy—a moment here, a moment there. That was why I understood a motorcycle.

I delivered my paper, *The Bi-Marginality of Design in the Construct of Motorcycle Fabrication*, at a multicultural conference at Montana State University at Billings and received a crowd around me. Afterwards, I went to the Yellowstone Art Museum. In the museum I saw an albumen print, *Standing Holy*, the daughter of Sitting Bull, taken by David Francis Berry, 1854–1934. But when did Standing Holy live? What were her dates? How did she stand holy as her people were slaughtered? As her world was turned inside out and she saw a program she didn't want to see. What would she do as her children and grandchildren intermarried with the comers in an unholy mix? What did she do with the nonfit she felt in this world that replaced the one she knew? Did she handle it like my father? Or did she stand firm in the old ways? He stood firm, my father, in his desperation. He never got a job the way my grandfather said he should. He stood firm to what he was. In that, he stood holy, though it made him a failure in my grandfather's eyes. Maybe it was more than I had done. I lived a traitor to what I knew or felt sometimes when I woke in the morning and heard the old world of my father and knew why he ran from this one.

My vision for you all, dear students, is that you hold firm. *Stand Holy.* It's why walnuts are pounded flat and shaped into wood that is cut into furniture with a knobbed head and foot rail, so the little walnuts can become lovely furniture that is sold for nothing and passed onto others at a grandmother's death.

# GRADY AND GUS

A horse is from the sky, which a dream is.

A horse speaks a language we don't know—

to hear a horse-song is to hunger for the words beyond knowing.

Grady—

Something comes from my dreams like an animal I can't see, but pulls me on the ground. I'm walking blindfolded. I dream of Gus every night. He's saying something. His mouth moves but there're no words.

I dream of a horse mask. I tell you, man, I was back there. Farther than we can remember. It's was great-grandpa or great-great-grandpa making horse masks. It's all there—buffalo hide and horns, porcupine quills, pony beads. There were horses in a field. They wore spotted dresses. They were wounded in battle.

Not dresses—those tunics or long shirts the Taliban wear. The ones that shot you—they waited in that building.

Shot by someone wearing a dress, man. I wasn't paying attention. What did we know but car-jacking—and riding horses not ours—

If you're in trouble one more time—you'll find yourself in combat uniform and desert camouflage.

They're grinding us into the ground, man.

Sometimes I have a hunger for something—I don't have a name for it. It's a hunger beyond which a name is waiting. If I could get there to see the name—to name it with the name—I would know what it is. But I can't get through the hunger without a name. I don't have the name to get to the name—

What're you talking about?

A no-name-hunger—a nameless hunger that can't be filled.

Then say it like it is.

I can't speak Crow. English tripped us up. In grade school, those teachers had hedge trimmers—those huge scissors they used to cut off our heads. Or the words that came out of our heads. Or the thoughts that were formed in our heads. No—the way our heads formed our thoughts—

We don't have hedges on the reservation, man. That's a way to get around hedge trimmers.

How long did it take me to learn to be quiet? How long did it take me to realize I was supposed to be invisible?

We'll tell the judge we're signing up. Serve our country. It beats reading books.

It beats picking Elroon's blackberries—selling them by the road. My hands itch thinking about it. How'd grandma do it?—bending over those bushes all those years picking those little sniper beasts? Those blackberry bullets. What an arsenal those bushes were. What you think?

We stepped into another world. Tell me a story.

Horses in a field—Appaloosas. Their spots hand-painted on their flanks.

They're with us, man, on this fucking tour-of-duty.

The first time the Indian saw a horse, he called it, elk dog.

Holy dog.

At one time, the sun rode across the sky on a horse.

I'm afraid of the Taliban. It's their land, man. You know that gives them power.

Did it give the Indians power when the cavalry rode in? I ripped the sleeve of my shirt the first time we crawled under the barbed-wire fence to ride the ponies.

In those days, they removed tonsils. In those days, they used ether—Count backwards—10 9 8 7 6 5 4 3 2 1—and I was asleep.

Once a man had a dream—If he stood under the sky with a magic rope, he could catch the animal that passed there. It was an animal he'd never seen. But if he made a rope and stood under the sky—the rope would become magic, and he could catch the animal. The man threw his lasso into the air, and was jerked to the ground, and dragged a long way, until he said, whoa. And the horse obeyed.

Our people were horse raiders. We still go to Hardin and drive away with someone's car.

We ride into Afghanistan and take their donkey and horse carts. Pow. Pow. Wow.

If I stand under the sky with a rope I'll find a horse.

Our horses are Humvees.

When a storm comes, the horses run. It's the desert sand that blows. The horses lift the edges of the earth and let hell out.

War horses don't run away in battle.

I fell off a horse the first time I tried to ride. I got the wind knocked out of me. I was on the ground trying to suck air back into my lungs. Dad stood over me laughing. When I could breathe, I got up, and tried to kick him, but he held me away from him with his hand on my head.

You always had a temper, Gus.

I used it against you.

I don't remember.

You remember. I scared the hell out of you, man. Myself too.

Shut up, soldier. Keep your eye on those buildings ahead.

Stinking wrong-headed war.

We should have stayed in school.

My throat's closed off, but I'm talking. Grady, listen to me with your fucking ears. What are you yelling about?

He's hit in the throat. What's taking Medic so long?

Remember when we walked blindfolded? I held my eyes closed. I didn't need a blindfold. But you couldn't be trusted to keep your eyes closed.

You tied the kerchief high on my forehead, Gus. I could see my feet moving on the ground.

It'll be the same in Kandahar, man. Only the sergeant'll tell us what to do.

Those little thorns on the blackberry bushes were invisible. I couldn't see them until they stuck in my fingers. They were like steel-wool filings on Uncle Zebo's work table. Little devils. You'd scream when grandma'd pick the thorns out.

I wanted to carry combat gear on my back. I never had anything more than what I could fit in a duffle bag—Jeans. Shirt. Socks and underwear. A parka and snow boots.

We won't need snow boots there.

Let's go to the field—tell the Appaloosas we'll see them later.

Maybe they'll come with us—War should be returned to horse-back.

Fort Leonard Wood, Missouri. Ten-weeks basic combat training. Drills. Formations. Marching. Red, white and blue phases from patriot to gunfighter to warrior.

Oakley combat boots. Camouflage suits. Shaved heads.

What would Lindy, Ruth Annie and Shane think of us?

Shauna—Gus always corrected me. I don't know why you can't remember her name.

Hand to hand combat. Weapons manual. Grenade launchers. MZ50 caliber heavy machine gun. Night-vision goggles.

I will never quit. I will never accept defeat.

Gas mask. Jabbing with bayonet. GPS. M60 machine gun.

Run, soldier, with 40 pounds on your back.

Rifle, sidearm, combat knife, grenade, water canteen, food-pack, amo, ear plugs. Now you got something else in your back pack.

Gus somewhere between Afghanistan and Montana with an Elder—

I'm making a horse mask.

My throat hurts.

You were shot in the neck.

I nearly died, man.

Now you have.

I want to go back. Grady's my brother.

You can't—but you still can fight.

There's war here?

Yes, this is the cooling tank. You've got to face your wounds. See, I paint your horse-mask half-blue and half-red with hail-spots on its forehead that look like stars.

There're healing ceremonies for soldiers returning from war.

There're ceremonies for those who don't.

I saw a horse in a dream.

This is the one you saw. This is your healing story.

I haven't heard of a ceremony like this.

You haven't been in a place like this. Your grandfathers always were fighting for you. Battling with death over you. Others wanted to let you go. The times you drove drunk.

I see Appaloosas in a field.

You'll hear a horse song in a dream.

Look at the Montana fields—barley and oats. The round moon shining like a yard-light in the distance. I see Lindy's house. I thought death would be different.

Whad you think what it would be like?

I didn't think. Maybe I hoped it would feel like riding the Appaloosa.

The horse that wasn't yours?—after the rancher told you boys to stay out of his pasture.

Yes, that one. But this's different. I used to hate the rez. Just destroy myself and others in the car. That was the destination, though we didn't want to know it. What's that taste?

Pemmican—the blackberries your grandmother pounded with dried buffalo meat for your journey.

What else in the back pack?

It's a medicine bundle. A stone from the Little Bighorn River on the Crow reservation.

The ones I used to collect?

The one you threw at Grady when he had to have six stitches in his head.

I saw the scar when the army shaved his head.

There's the wing-bone of a bird—and a feather in the medicine bundle.

Probably the bird I killed with my first b-b gun.

The bird that called to you the mornings you didn't want to go to school and your father carried you screaming to the bus.

What else in the bundle? A spark plug?

From the last car you stole from Hardin.

Do you keep note of all my sins?
That's someone else's job.


Lindy from Beauxwuaashe near the Crow Agency in Montana—
I saw Gus gear up. I saw the excitement in his eyes. There
was fear there too. Maybe it was part of the excitement. He loved
to steal into someone's pasture and ride the horses. He always
wanted danger. He loved his army gear even before he had it. He
was in love with war—with going to war. He loved talking about
war. Thinking about it. His bravery. His defense of his country. It
was a world I couldn't be part of—Gus already was married to the
army—to war. A soldier's wife is war. There wasn't room for me. I
couldn't argue and say, stay with me. When we were together, war
stepped between us. A soldier's children are war. A soldier has no
family other than war. I was in his way. He had to step past me to go
to war. War is their field. Their truth. Their universe. Their blind-
spot. I saw war in his eyes. Destroy the enemy, whoever they are.
Whoever you are taught they are. I saw war come upon him. When
he came back from combat training before deployment, Gus was
at war. Gus was war. I hear war in the hinges of the pasture gate. It
was my own screaming. War is the pulley. War is the hay lifted into
the barn loft. Gus is stored somewhere above me now—returning
on a cargo plane—over my head—where it all is. What is it like in
a coffin draped with a flag?


What is war? Where does it come from? It lives in a man's head.
Maybe it's more in the heart. It lives first in the imagination—
wherever that is.


The government sent Gus back to us in a box draped with a flag.
We went to the airport in Billings in a convoy to bring him back
to the reservation. Lindy was shaking with sobs. She's always
been that way—she'd get hysterical if she saw a dog with a rabbit
squirming in its mouth. That's the way it is. My chief grief with the
army—War absorbs a man. War doesn't give them back. Not the

men we knew anyway. War makes a mark on them that doesn't go away. A man stays in the war. Even with the ceremonies for his journey to the next world—the burning of sage to clean Gus from the death he went through—Those elders hosed him down with their words. The coffin remained closed. We couldn't see him. How did we know it was him? How did we know he wasn't riding a horse somewhere in Afghanistan?—that he decided to stay there. Maybe it was better than the reservation. You can imagine Lindy with her tears. Screeching like a rabbit. What did Gus have to return to? He was not going to make it in school. He saw the road narrow. He saw too many doomed with alcohol. What could he do? He thought about places he could go. That's how Gus and Grady began thinking of the army.

Grady wounded in the leg in Afghanistan—

Watch it, Grady!!—

Dear Ruth—Kandahar, Afghanistan. Dear Annie—On patrol in night-vision goggles. Dear Shauna—the tree looks like it's wrapped in chartreuse duct-tape—

Medic!! Man down. Grady's wounded.

I see a storm on the plains—from clear across the world. Shauna's at the house by herself. She's probably not paying attention. Or if she is, she's afraid.

What're we doing at Unlce Zebo's with his steel-wool filing down gun barrels and serial numbers?

Every time I close my eyes, I'm a soldier running and running. I felt myself running when I was shot. I felt myself running after I was wounded. How could the soldiers tourniquet a leg that was running? I ran when I was strapped on the gurney. I ran when I heard the helicopter. My brother was shot in the neck. Now I was shot in the leg.

I imagined an Appaloosa as I ran. I ran and ran until I took its mane in my hands. I jumped on its back. I ran with Gus in the truck on the Crow Rez. It's snowing!—There's a white-out on the road ahead of us, Gus. You can't see where you're going. We got one lane through the snow. Slow down, Gus. The air is full of fuzz.

What if someone's coming from the other way? We can't see their headlights until it's too late. What if a spirit's standing in the road? Remember the stick figures we saw near the Little Bighorn down the road from our place?—

A plane runs in the sky with its legs folded up.

I can't see where I'm running.

I see the plane—its legs unfold as it gets ready to land.

It sounds like incoming ground fire.

What do we know about ground fire? What do we know about shrapnel incoming like a pack of rez dogs?

We ran in the winter when the ground was covered with hoar frost. Remember, Gus—the old ones that came in the cold? We saw them cross the field.

I used to watch the moon walk away from my window.

Those mornings the air was frozen and sparked with ice.

Once Gus fell and thought his leg was broken. One of the old ones came and touched his leg with a medicine stick. Did that happen? Am I imagining it? Couldn't the old ones travel to Afghanistan? Can't they go anywhere?

The trees were covered with white frost. I used to draw their stick figures in the frost on the window pane. They looked like the old ones standing there.

The teacher gave me a pencil one year and Gus broke it. I'm sorry, Gus. You were like Uncle Zebo sometimes—always looking for something hurtful—whamming us with snowballs.

You were always ahead of me in everything. Even death.

I thought the hardest snowballs came from Uncle Zebo. I think now they came from you.

Sometimes in those storms—when there was thunder—I thought I heard the battlefield. The soldiers at the Little Bighorn— when they saw they were surrounded.

I wrote in my Big Chief Tablet—Shauna loves Grady.

I wrote, Annie loves Grady.

I wrote, Grady loves Ruth.

I cried when Gus died. I screamed after him when they carried him away. A medic was there holding me back. Cry, soldier.

He said. Cry. I broke into pieces of grief. I was mad at Gus—for dying on me. He was shot. There was nothing I could do to bring him back. But there was more—underneath the grief was anger. You were mean, Gus. That's what I want to tell you. You hit me when we were kids. You scared me. The faster I ran from you, the slower I went. Gus. You're kicking my bed again.

I'm running—There's nothing ahead—the road is barren as the land I just returned from.

Dad's out there yelling—I had two sons who went to war. The government took them for their battle. My sons made their war machines. One dead. The other wounded—

Does a soldier return from war? A combat soldier's always on his toes.

I don't want to share you with Ruth and Annie.

It keeps you on your toes, baby.

Just because you're injured—you think you got something to hide behind. Who can compete with your injury?

Nobody who hasn't been there doesn't have the right to say what I got to hide behind.

You're right, Grady. While you were in the field of danger, I was standing in my little house baking cookies.

While you were in your kitchen, I was in Afghanistan's Easy Bake—heated by a high-watt light bulb. Every day—115°.

Gus is dead. Grady's wounded in the leg. He's wounded inside his head where it's hard to see. You need night-vision goggles to see where he's hurt.

We all know one another, Grady. I see you with Shauna or Ruth in your truck. You might want to make a decision.

I like to spread it around.


Annie's life as an invisible girl—

Sometimes I see a girl dancing in a jingle dress and I grieve. I want to go back and start again. I want to be that girl. I could inhabit her body. I could suck her out of her arms and legs and take her place. I don't want to go down the road I followed. I want another road. I would not end up nowhere. Once in a while,

I see something, and those old days come back. I want to go to my grandmother's house and sit with her on her sagging couch and watch the old black & white Zenith—those tv programs that came and went according to which way the wind was blowing. We were out there in the country past Lodge Grass and the whole sky turned over us with its stars. We were part of the universe. There was danger. A stranger could come. An Indian drunk with a zipping rage—a desperation beyond reach. A pack of animals could scratch down the door.

A war is never over. It just moves someplace else.

Look at the sky. How will I know where Gus has gone? I'll sink into darkness.

Those little stars are windows. You'll see where to go once you're there. Stay with us for now, Grady.

There's a plane up there so far, it hisses.

I ran from the dog that used to chase us. He had the shortest legs and longest tail of any rez mutt. He'd throw himself against the truck when we passed.

I ran after you, Grady.

I ran as if I was smoke rising from a brush fire. Higher and higher into the finishing-line of the sky.

I used to sit in my closet. A thin strip of light under the door. A few dresses hanging on the gallows above me—most of them too small. I didn't have more than a change of clothes. One pair of shoes.

Lindy's chartreuse duct tape is the flash of gun-fire through my night-vision goggles. I can't go, Ruth. We got to turn back. I'm afraid of a road-side bomb.

A road-side bomb on highway 451? All we got here are deer crossings.

Stop, Ruth. STOP!! It's about to blow.

Grady—you're crazy!! This isn't Afghanistan. Don't panic. You're safe.

Army manual. Old Soviet land mines. Nothing is known. All is hidden. Hidden and moving. We're targets. We're dust and hashish. The Taliban let us have it. I want base camp. Small village compound. Squatted against the wall. Sitting on their heels. I.E.D.s. Screech of rockets. Bezzelled in duct tape.


Lindy at Montana State—

Gus left me hanging here. What can I do?—Go to art class. Make a day of it. The art teacher saw the repairs I made on Gus' jean jacket. He asked what else I could do with duct tape. We took a trip to Walmart. There were rolls of duct tape—camouflage duct tape, duct tape with flames, duct tape with hail-spots, duct tape with stripes. Every pattern I could imagine. I made a duct tape parfleche. I made head-bands with camouflage duct tape. I made regalia of sorts—bustle, roaches. I made duct tape neckties. Gus would never wear a tie. I made spirit patterns. I called them, Arrows-for-someone-who-goes-away-and-never-comes-back. I made duct tape covers for my books. I made a gallows rope. After Little Bighorn College, I went to Montana State University in Billings. The other girls followed. Gus was even there a few weeks—before the army. Grady followed him too. Sometimes I think Gus is still here. I'm going to make a horse mask of duct tape. I dreamed about it last night.

I heard my dad out in the yard scraping ice from the windshield of his old truck. He went to work each morning to provide for us. His scraping sounded like a rodent in the wall of our house. Moving place to place. Scratching here. Scratching there. He brought the horses into the barn in a terrible blizzard. There would have been no way to get to them with hay. The barn was alive with stock and horses. Their breath. The shuffling of their feet. Their noises. In the dark, in the lantern light, there was a glow that lifted from the animals. Something was there. I wanted to stay with them in the barn. My dad carried me crying back to the house. Maybe it was the first time I felt that hunger for something that wasn't mine. The animals had a world they lived in. Maybe I wanted the world where we once had lived with them.

Gus went to Afghanistan. Gus died there. A long time ago, he kissed me behind the barn before I knew what that kind of kiss meant. It must have been sixth grade. In high school, he took me home. He had his mother's truck. She was tired of coming to get them. Grady sat shot-gun. I saw Shauna, Ruth, Annie glare at me as I left riding between them. I like Shauna, Grady. She'd be the one for a wife. You're going to have to stop dating three women at the same time.

What if it takes three women to take care of me? My wounds make me angry. I'd wear one woman out.

I went to the place where Gus and I used to park. I thought I could meet him there. I believe in ghosts. I believe the past is still with us. But all that was there was the land. Sometimes I smell sage. I think the old ones are making an offering. Maybe Gus is with them.

Those stick figures are trees in the ravine by the creek. The dead don't come back.

Gus could get along without the night light, Lindy, Grady said. We don't need to go to the cemetery.

I found the glow-lights at Walmart. I don't want him out here in the dark.

Gus doesn't know it's dark. He's not here.

Part of him is.

Why are cemetery gravestones in even rows? Why do they stand in a military formation? They should be random—like the constellations—

Let him go, Grady. Each day you seem heavier—not weight, but you're sinking. Each day you belong more to Gus. He's pulling you underground. I'll be coming to the cemetery with a night light for you, Grady. You'll be out here in the cold.

I was talking to Gus when the bullet went through his throat. It caught Gus because he turned to look at me. He made a motion as if he was going to nudge me, and the bullet hit. I saw him fall. I watched the blood soak through the rag we tried to hold at his neck until medic got there. I called him and called him. Don't leave me, Gus. Who else do I have?

Your father.

I always was afraid of him. Gus was more a father—

Gus was mean too. He told me he used to kick his foot against your mattress in the bunk bed and send you flying.

Gus—
I want to be on the rez with Lindy and Grady. Grady's tonsils are gone. My throat is gone. I am standing. I am falling. I see a horse with a red and blue head marked with stars. I see it coming from the sky. My name on its thigh. Wads of seed from the cotton-wood tied to its hooves. I see horses stand on the hill with riders. They wear horse-head masks. They hold horse-dance sticks. They're with us, Grady.

He can't see them.

That doesn't mean they aren't there.

What have the people got in Afghanistan but war? It's their mission. There's nothing else for them. Could they plow hayfields in the sand? Soldiers keep appearing. They're like the cavalry—no matter what the grandfathers did, there were more soldiers the next day.

The storm I saw on the plains moves across the world. The clouds morph into blackberries. The blackberries morph into hail. The hail has sharpened thorns pounding and pounding. What hurts?—the thorns on those blackberry bushes?

Shrapnel. You're reliving your wounds to get back through them.

I'm standing on my toes trying to see over the world. I see the long Indian wars with Indians. The wars with Europeans. I see the Mankato uprising—the Indians hanging on the scaffolding, trying to stand on their toes to reach the ground. The wars of America with other countries. I don't want to see.

You have to look.

When Lindy pulls a strip of duct tape from its roll, I hear a helicopter. A helicopter rolls out of the sky like duct tape. Everything hangs on it.

A helicopter comes from the distance with the drone of traffic on I-90. At night in Afghanistan, when everything was quiet, we could hear the interstate. The trucks passing there—somehow the air carried the sound of their passing. Gus said once, it must have been like the sound of buffalo our great-grandfathers heard across the land—beyond one knoll or another. How could we hear the interstate—all the way in Afghanistan?

Geese honk in the sky over the fields in Montana. They fly sometimes at night. An incoming helicopter shakes the air. A helicopter sounds more like a crow squawking from the telephone poles. How can a helicopter be a goose and a crow?

There's a river on the res—the Little Bighorn—with fish where the deer and bear and coyote come to drink—it isn't a fast river—has anyone drowned? No, we couldn't step across it, but made a raft of a few pieces of scrap lumber and drifted out into the current that barely swept us along. We were oars-men. We were ropers. We were Indians with nowhere to go but war.

# SOMETHING CALLED
# ALMOST GOD

Wherefore it is said in the book of the wars of the Lord

—NUMBERS 21:14

# Chapter One

He could bang his head all day and they would not notice.

The girls sang with their voices saying, Let the redeemed say so, in a low, dreary voice without harmony—all on the same note—sounding like a recording in slow motion.

Brother Zebulun's prophecies—bees would invade, though it was known that bee colonies were disappearing, and they seemed to be growing fewer in number—Brother Z thought they were gathering somewhere to plan their invasion.

He also thought a fierce angel was buried in the desert it was so fierce. The giver of war and death. Angel O. But even the bad could be used for good, Brother Z said once. Though Wyatt didn't think it could.

No one would help Wyatt with his galoshes. No one covered his ears in the cold wind. At night, he felt there was a tiny bee eating his ear drum. He cried in pain and they lashed him. The lashes seem to come at random. He couldn't tie the punishment to what he had done. Why was he punished if his ear hurt?

He opened boxes he imagined were his. A toy soldier with arms. A ball.

As a baby he was bathed with hands that could hold him underwater as long as they wanted. And if he cried he went under again. Until he gave up. Until it did no good to cry.

His ears were open to the cold again. The pain in his head had a knife cutting into it. The bees were burrowing there for the winter. The other boys would see him sniveling in front of them. How loud would he cry if they poked the bruise on his head?

The men who were the custodians in the field wore hats with earflaps tied under their chins. They had long coats and scarves around their necks. Gloves on their hands.

Wyatt walked to a ledge by the reservoir—just a narrow walkway between the pools of water—he could fall anytime. He knew what it was to be underwater. To humiliate him, to erase himself from them.

Which would he face? The pain in his ear or the derision of the boys?

## Chapter Two

What Wyatt remembered—

The Book of the Wars of the Lord, though lost, probably was praise for what the Lord did for those who feared him. Wherefore it is said in the Book of the Wars of the Lord, what he did in the Red Sea and in the books of Arnon, where someone who would not let Israel pass on their way to the Promised Land was defeated.

Paul Clements was the neighbor down the road. His wife left hoe-cakes along the fence that bordered the All Saints Orphanage. She left them for the boys unless it was snowing or there was freezing drizzle that would ruin them.

It was a voice coming across the field. He could take a cake if he wanted.

It was a voice he saw as light, waking from the night. A barely visible light moving past the window of the Clements' house as if the voice held burning coals. Why couldn't the Clements take him? It was a question he could not think to ask, but remained half-thought-out in his head.

Let the redeemed say so.

What was the redeemed?

He could get in trouble asking that question. He should already know after all the sermons and Sunday school lessons and class lessons.

He had a power ranger they gave him one year with a battery pack still on its back. The battery didn't work. An arm had broken off in one fight, and the other arm in another. Wyatt slept with it against his face.

No one wanted it, but they resented his attachment to it.

Nothing should matter to anyone at All Saints.

Their eyes were on their heavenly home.

Their happy heavenly home in the hereafter.

He started writing all the words that began with h. Hallelujah. Horse. Heaven. Did horses go to heaven? The old ones in the meadow that could no longer work and just stood there staring at the air hardly moving all day as if dead already. Their swayed backs and bony legs could no longer work pulling a load, or carrying anything, not even a bag of corn.

Sometimes at night, he heard gunshot, and knew there would be one less old horse in the meadow.

A hoe-cake was a fried cornmeal flatbread. Flat as the girls singing in the orphanage. He thought of them as flat bread. He listened to their flat-voiced singing. It was flat as the world from the orphanage window.

They never knew where they were going until they got there. There were worse orphanages. Children had died in some of them.

In summer, they worked in the fields until the sun fried their skin. And cried at night with blisters from their burns.

In winter, their skin was blistered with cold.

Once, Mrs. Clements stood at the fence while Wyatt ate. She said a hoe-cake was made with cornmeal, hot water or milk, flour, baking powder and salt. It was kneaded and shaped with the palms. Honed by the hands.

You can take another cake. It was Mrs. Clements' voice.

## Chapter Three

What Wyatt forgot—

Here come bees—Brother Zebulun imagined. Right araund the corner of the buildin' our forefathers put up near fifty yar ago.

The squallin' bees comin'. Brother Zebulun swatted at the invisible swarm during the practice for the invasion of the bees. We have power over livin' beings. Even bees.

They comin' after hoe-cakes, Rubita, Brother Z's wife, said. Throwd 'em out just to call the bees to swell up your face so you cain't talk. She was angry Wyatt had one of Mrs. Clements' hoe-cakes.

## Chapter Four

It was the Sanderput brats that were the consternation of Wyatt. Two of them were in his class. One born at the beginning of a year. The other at the last. The other grades were full of other Sanderputs so the fifth grade kept the two of them that were the same ages three months out of the year. Beckon on that.

It was coming and going. The school days met him each morning. He took his books and walked to the school, just outback of the main building of the orphanage. The clapboard church was the other building, which also had been a barracks. Brother Zebulun's house was beyond that. Then a side meadow that reached the Clements' yard where the hoe-cakes disappeared at the fence.

Wyatt thought he could see Mrs. Clements looking from behind her curtain to make sure it was the orphans and not the rodents getting her hoe-cakes.

They read in school to see who could have the most chapters read. Until he knew they weren't reading, but making up the story as they looked at the page. It was the story of the feeding of the 5000 fish.

Brother Zebulun kept them after school again.

Years later, Wyatt remembered Mrs. Clements' face. He knew he would see her in the High Heaven of the Hereafter. He wouldn't be there, but he could look up and see her still passing out hoe-cakes.

Originally, hoe-cakes were baked on a hoe over an open fire for the field workers, she said. They were made from wheat or oat cereal boiled in water. Plain as gruel. Without milk or eggs. Just boiled water and some meal.

Years later, when he spent his December salary on hoe-cakes for the children, and brought them to the All Saints Orphanage, he could hear the old voices of the girls. Let the redeemed say so.

Did they know up there on the ceiling angels counted the welts on the children?

## Chapter Four

She raised her arm. Get!! Rubita, Brother Z's wife, said. The bull looked at her. The rabbit stood in the yard ready to run, but preferred to chew grass. The bull turned slowly, belligerently, as if thinking of something so important he wasn't aware of her. As if some inner thought called him away, but then he turned and gored her.

Wyatt could hear Brother Zebulun yelling at the heavens for help.

Wyatt ran as far as he could without stopping. Even after he heard the sirens. Then fell by the side of the road gulping for breath. In the air, he heard the footsteps—Angel O, the angel of death, not buried in the desert after all—with its wings opened wide, letting go of the bee invasion it held back as long as it could.

# THE SERVITUDE OF LOVE

Joanna the Mad

1479-1555

Tengo que hablaros de el—I must speak of him

Philip wouldn't know me now.

Todos nos marchitamos como hojas—We fade as a leaf. Almost fifty years in the convent after his death. What madness is here. The leaves in the heavy air hiss. Santa Clara Convent, Tordesillas, Spain—mi manicomio—my asylum.

The 2nd daughter of Ferdinand of Aragon and Isabella of Castile. I married Philip the Handsome at 16 in 1495. My sister, Catherine of Aragon, married Henry VIII.

I am mad with love. In that, they are correct. Love is a madness. Love did not die with Philip, but lives to rage. I know nothing but him, and he knew nothing but women. No, I don't want to be sane. I want to be Juana la Loca—DEMENTE por AMOR—Insane with love—Yes—I am in love with madness.

I went with a fleet from Spain to Flanders to marry the Archduke Philip of Burgundy. The only son of Maximilian of the Holy Roman Empire. He sent his sister, Margaret, to meet the ship. But when he saw me, he ordered us married immediately. Hardly the vows were out of my mouth but he carried me away. He took off my clothing and I knew love in his bed.

Our three ships were lost on the way to Flanders—I wanted to tell him. A month of sea waves. Tossing and sickness. How much longer—this trip? I paced the deck. I spit at the wind. Thousands traveled with me. I didn't speak his language. But I knew his eyes. Be quiet—they said. Open your mouth only for love.


Hojarascas nos rodean—Fallen leaves surround us.

We are going forth. Venom of devils. Women carry their bones—This is the message. The warning. The nuns say they come for singing. But they come for war. The leaves are their sad victims. I didn't know trees cried until I was locked in the convent.

It is where I heard them. It is where I came to know their secret. The nuns made their little wars on the leaves they kept in the convent. The leaves tried to wedge themselves between the bars to escape, but they were locked in.

My catapult also was at the convent wall. My mangonel. Yet they thwart all attempts to escape. The little nuns torture us on their racks. They carry weapons. They would let no one speak to me.

I chortled. Unable to move. I could not sleep. The nuns wanted to kill me. I knew their intent. I could not lift my arm into my sleeve. They waited upon me, holding my arm in the air. I could not lift my fork from my plate. My spoon from my bowl. Sometimes my daughter fed me until she went off to that crazy place—marriage—that torture pit when a man ties your heart to the rack and stretches it until it cannot be recognized as a heart.

I hear them from the window of Santa Clara Convent—There are leaves to rake. The nuns are practicing now. They have a commission of some kind to work. Their fingers cracked. I raged in my sleep. I woke dragging it with me. Who was he looking at now? Who was he kissing?

## Infancia

My tutors, Antonio and Allisandro Gerardino, taught me Latin and geography. I liked to sit with them and study. I was mad for my father too, throwing my arms around his neck when I was a child, kissing and kissing. My mother was remote. She kept her feelings to herself. Her mother, Isabel of Portugal, brought madness to the family. She left her impression. My mother would have nothing to do with it. She would have nothing to do with anything that obscured reason.

These were the children of my parents—Ferdinand of Aragon and Isabella of Castile—Isabella of Castile, 1470–1498. Juan,

1478–1497. Joanna of Castile, 1479–1555. Maria of Aragon, 1482–1517. Catherine of Aragon, 1485–1536.

We ran through the corridors. We were scolded if she heard us. We saw how quiet and how fast we could run. Juan always won, but he was older. Isabella, my older sister, was slow. I could nearly win.

My parents loved geography. I heard talk of the unknown world. They loved to imagine voyages across the boiling sea. GEOGRAFIA. OCEANO. TIERRA. I yelled the words from my window until they came and stopped me.

I learned to be surmised. Scrutinized. When I saw Philip, I didn't care what anyone saw. I was still reeling from the ship's ride when I saw him looking at me. What did he expect? Some dowdy toad? Some pale frump? Mujer desalineada?

I learned horsemanship as a girl. Philip was a lover of horses. It was the meaning of his name. Amante de los caballos. He kissed my flanks. He brushed my mane. He was proud of me. Then I saw all the women conspiring against me for him—for just one afternoon with him—until I was jealous, suspicious, paranoid.

How close we came to flying. How close to the birds. Their business in the leaves. Their work. Their oblivion to our needs. They are workers in their little industrious world. Did they care for my agony?

When we were girls, we played, Married to a King. Our servants laced us up in starched camisoles and dresses made of silk and embroidery. We were flotillas, crying, Casadacon un Rey. Later, we were trussed up. Corseted. Staved. Hooked and tied. Hosed. Headdressed. Ruffed and sleeved. It didn't seem a voyage then. But marooned on a dock.

## Honed of its Wedginess

One day, Philip had a headache. I found him in bed by himself. I heard no feet hurrying down the hall. No quick pulling up of covers. I smelled the bed. There had been no woman there. But I recognized the smell of an intruder—Sickness. I was angrier than if it was a woman.

Philip became feverish. He couldn't sleep. He had a nose bleed. He ached. He suffered chills. He couldn't swallow. He couldn't speak, though I saw the anger in his silence.

I called his men to pull him up. NOW!! He sat up a moment before falling back. They tried again at my command. Philip was able to sit another moment, but sank back down into the bed. It was then I saw the red marks—splots of roses crossed his chest. I wanted to bury my nose in them. The women pulled me back. I was carrying our sixth child. Stand back. It would bring harm. Beware—But I had been beware of this man since I first saw him. Other women eyed him. I lived with their infernal glares. They turned their eyes when they saw my evil look at them.

I screamed at the doctors. I don't want to live without HIM. He's been POISONED by FERDINAND, my father, who hated him. No, they denied. Maybe Philip suffered from typhoid AND poison. My father had his hand in it. He sent his secret emissaries. Poison, I insisted. Typhoid, the doctors determined. ENVEN-ENADO y tifoidea.

A doctor bled Philip. The monks prayed for him. Priests. Holy fathers. Wart removers and witches. All. I heard the leaves hiss. I thought I heard the birds praying. I had the servant pour out more grain for them. The rooster and chickens. The cows and goats. The ticks and weevils.

Philip went over the margin of the sea in the void. I heard stories from his ship. The typhoon. The hurricane. All of them nothing in the face of typhoid. The fever. GET RID OF IT, I screamed. They tried to quiet me. There was another child inside me. Couldn't I consider it?—they begged. I was haunted with Philip. I was him. Then I heard—El Archiduque esta MUERTO!!

I was blistering. I was thwarted.

Philip DEAD at the age of 28?—He left me behind in a storm of grief. I felt like I was crossing an ocean to him—seasick with a child.

I kept Philip with me a week after he died. I caressed his body, as though my love could bring life to him again. I had his coffin opened several times. Not to pull him out, but to reassure myself he was there. There was rumor his body had been taken from me.

They said I could not keep him with me. But I was Queen. They did what I said. Love can do anything. Madly, love can reign. I remained a madfly they could do nothing with. I roamed the halls. I called Philip's name. I thought he was hiding behind the curtains. I doubled over with childbirth. I howled. I tried to go after him.

One day, the soldiers came and removed me to another place—WHERE IS THIS? I screeched. The baby screeched with me, but the wagon kept rattling over the road. Santa Clara, they said. A NUNNERY??? I watched the ugly, warted guard. I told him so.

I was sturdy as the ocean. Morbid. Obsessed the death. I burned with Philip's love.

Fifty years confined at the Santa Clara Convent in Tordesillas near Valladolid, Spain, in the same room. I kept my youngest daughter, Catherine, with me in an adjoining room. She looked from her window all day. Until she too was married.


# Expedicion

When I was thirteen, my parents, Ferdinand and Isabella, sat Christopher Columbus in the Santa Maria, the Nina and the Pinta, going over the waves. My parents liked exploration. They talked wildly of voyages and journeys to the New World that was there on the other side of the water. They liked exploration because it brought back wealth to Spain. I heard my father, Ferdinand, talking when he didn't know I was under the chair that was his throne in the council room.

Love started with a ship to the unknown. There was a wedge somewhere—the ships could fall. They sent the expendable ones toward it. What a joyous trip of despair.

I was Queen of Spain, Mexico, Peru and the Caribbean Islands, and they came to whip me in Santa Clara Convent. If I raged, I was beat. If I was beat, I raged. The train of my robe was the stars of the open sea. The twags. Hammer-heads. In the convent's infernal silence. Their slurping of porridge. Their chewing of a slice of carrot. Their gratefulness for nothing. Don't the nuns ever scream?

I heard the little clicks of their shoes on the stones like kissing sounds—like sound made from love. What did they know of anything? What exploration had they made but the misery of their lot?

These interior passages to madness I traveled 100 times a day. I was a ship on the sea. I was the underwater terror that waited. I was the storm that pushed the boat into the hills of waves that came against it. I was the suck beneath it.

I frayed the end of my sash. It was wet with saliva. You aren't trying to eat it, are you? They asked.

I was an old woman still frying with love.

I dragged my sashes behind me. I bellowed like a cow. My bellowings echoed through the convent. The nuns hovered together in a corner lest the madness of love overtake them. I hear their prayers. Their sayings. Sus hojas jamas se marchitan—His leaf shall not wither—Psalm 1:3.

## Anulada

Henry exiled Catherine, my youngest sister, after many years of marriage. She came to me sometimes in my cell, looking for her throne. It's not here, I said. At least you don't have to tie your head back onto your neck with a sash. How was it married to the King?

Who was the God who tortured us with men and their desires? She said.

No, I told her. I chose my own desire for Philip.

How is it there are such things as men with their power over us?

Was that the nuns' prayers each day?—That they see no man. That the desire for a man not take their hearts lest they be a raving lunatic like Joanna.

Sus hojas se marchitaran—The leaf shall be for medicine—
Ezekiel 47:12.

Bring me leaves, I ordered. I ate them until the nuns removed
them from me. Looking in my skirts. In my bodice. In the wedgi-
ness of the linings of my mouth. Removing all the leaves from me
even though I howled for them.

The nuns carry cartridges on their rosaries. They store grape-
shot behind the chapel. They sit in their mansuetude, but they are
crazy as men and their batty wars for power.

Do you hear how my thoughts scatter like the leaves? They
rake them into little piles, but the wind sweeps them across the
co $nvent yard. They sweep them back into piles, and they scatter
again.

I felt splats on my ability to reason. My continual outbursts
left their residue.

I was the daughter of a King and Queen. The wife of a King.
A Queen in my own right. The mother of Queens and a King. But
what was royal power when there was a mighty God who turned
me into the howl of a ship?

Who would have the power to hurt the other?—that was the
prayer of my family. My brothers and brothers-in-law, my sons and
sons-in-law, my uncles and distant cousins scrapped over it like
hunting dogs. I joined them. We ravished. Tore others into pieces.
A pile of burning leaves—all of us.

I was not mad. I was saner than any of them who committed
despicable acts in the name of power. The need to control was a
spur. A burr.

I was from the royal family of Hapsburg. My family wanted
my entitlement. I raged against them. I looked for the nun's arsenal. Their warehouse of weapons. They had me carried back to my
room.

## An Inquisition of Its Own

Typhos was the Conqueror, though it was a vapor. A fever. A
stupor. There was fever and intestinal disorder. Blood from his

bowels. I ordered no one to clean up after Philip but me. ME. His WIFE. He knew it now. My faithfulness. My obedience.

Because of Philip, I was Queen of one half of Belgium, France and the Netherlands. I was Queen of his Bed.

These children came from our love—Eleanor in 1498. Charles in 1500. Isabella in 1501. Ferdinand in 1503. Mary in 1505. Catherine was born after Philip died.

Typhus is a foil. A malaise. A nose bleed. An aching. It is paranoid as a Queen. These thoughts keep returning as waves on the sea—Philip died sedated. He died in delirium. How gross to be woven with the hot strands of love. How delirious. How detestable. How delicious. I wanted nothing but love.

I wailed at his funeral mass. Under my veil came a hand that covered my mouth. I bit at it. Another hand clamped my mouth. I heard a voice—the Queen would be removed from her seat in the church if she was not quiet. Then a cloth was tied across my mouth when they were tired of being bit.

The priests continued with their rites. Their endless words. What did they have to say about Philip that was louder than my grief?

What wickedness hides within us? What secrecy? What schemes and plans to steal? It was a mast on my head. An ocean in my belly.

I was afraid of a goiter. A fearsome beast at my neck. A servant in court had one and the servant was removed because of my screaming. I had my sisters scream also.

None of it pernicious as typhoid.

I chewed at the cloth they tied at my mouth until they carried me back to the convent.


I lay in my cell face down on the dusty floor. They often thought I was dead. I heard their whispering outside my room. Devoid as they were of their own lives. Just give them a night with Philip. They'd be on their knees the rest of their lives begging for more. They'd run from the convent. They'd abandon Christ.

Later the servant with a goiter haunted my dreams at the Santa Clara Convent.

Philip comes back in these storms. He returns daily. Time coils around itself out of order. I could not get over that voyage, but was tossed back upon it and upon it in the waves.

## Unas Vacaciones en Espana

At one time, early in our marriage, we went from Flanders to Spain. I left the children behind. Philip hated Spain. The heat. The hateful and accusing looks from my mother. My father's distrust.

Philip caught measles and when he was well enough to travel, he returned to Flanders, leaving me in Spain.

I was overwrought, my mother said. I remembered the groaning of the galley ship with the sea pushing against it. Squeezing it to the top of the water. These forces working against each other.

I was kept at Castle La Mota. On a cold November night, I fled without a cloak. When the gate closed before I could escape, I threw myself against the bars of the gate, SCREAMING, cursing, raising my fist against God. I would have the Bishop tortured and killed for keeping me imprisoned. I told him so. When my mother arrived, I yelled at her because she had ordered me locked up.

You're crazy as your grandmother—she slapped me. You're known by your frenzy.


Eventually, I returned to Flanders and my beloved Philip. When I saw his mistress, I cut off her hair. The little whimpet. Easy to hold down. To twist and writhe under me. She was no match for my fury. Philip would not come near her now.

A handsome man can do what he wants. When I saw him, I was in love. My passion tore him. No corsets. No warming pans. Just my loose sleeping gown open to the toes.

Now at Santa Clara Convent, I was paralyzed from the waist down. Ulcers bore upon my legs. I heard the darkness raging at the leaves. Madly. They pulled me from the tree. Who are you?—I am Joanna the wife of Philip.

Fondly. Darkness came. And the wedge off the end of the earth. Howling as an inquisition.

I was buried next to my husband in the royal chapel at Granada. We are side by side in our beds. No one comes between us.

Philip the Handsome 22 July 1478—25 September 1506

Joanna the Mad 6 November 1479—12 April 1555

At night I feel my hand reach across to him.